The Burning of The Piping Rock

Joseph Cutshall-King

matchless
books.

Library of Congress Number 2010919584

ISBN 978-1-60571-097-6

Embraceable You, © 1930 Music by George Gershwin and lyrics by Ira Gershwin; Alfred Publishing Co., Inc.

Jambalaya (On The Bayou); © 1952 Music and lyrics by Hank Williams, Sr.

Make Love To Me; Originally *The Tin Roof Blues,* © 1923 by Walter Melrose, lyricist; music by George Brunies, Paul Joseph Mares, Melville J. Stitzel, Leon Rappolo, and Ben Pollack (members of 'New Orleans Rhythm Kings'). The 1954 Four Lads' recording *Make Love to Me* had a new lyric added by Bill Norvas and Allan Copeland.

(The Gang that Sang) Heart of My Heart: © 1926 Music and lyrics by Ben Ryan

The Music Goes Round and Round; © 1935 Music and lyrics by Michael Riley, Edward Farley and William (Red) Hodgson.

First Edition, Second Printing

Cover design & all artwork © 2010 by Michael G. King, Black Swan Image Works, Westminster, Colorado

Printed in the United States of America by Shires Press, 4869 Main St., Manchester Center, VT

DEDICATION

This book is dedicated to my wife, Sara, who helped me make it a reality by believing in it and in me; and in memory of my late parents, George and Jane King.

THANKS

My sincerest thanks are given to several people who have helped immeasurably: The artist Michael G. King of Black Swan Image Works, who is also my brother, designed the wonderfully evocative cover and the colophon for the book. Also, his critique of my first draft led to my giving it a heavy, very much needed editing. William Lee Richards used his valuable experiences as a musician and WW II veteran to review the draft for period language. Author Peter Marino read the draft and offered welcomed advice. I was very fortunate to be able to have access to the collections of The Saratoga Room of the Saratoga Springs Public Library and the excellent help of its staff. In particular, historian Victoria Garlanda gave me many hours of priceless counsel on people, places and events in that time period of Saratoga's history. For providing the indispensable work of proofing for spelling and grammar my thanks go to Donna Bates, to my wife, Sara Cutshall-King, and to my daughter, Julia Cutshall-King. I am indebted to my late parents for the Saratoga history they confided to me, some of which is included here and more of which is not. And, finally, a tip of the hat goes to Harry for all the work he did and the inspiration he provided.

jack

Preface

Pharmacists are priests. They know how to keep secrets. George A. King, my father, was a pharmacist. He took all his secrets to his grave, except one: his secret of the burning of the Piping Rock Casino in Saratoga Springs, New York, on the night of August 16-17, 1954. He taped his confession just before he died. Whether he intended to or not, I am sharing it.

He died July 31, 1987. He left some major bills, some personal papers, and a dented Pontiac Phoenix I bought from his estate. Just before I sold it in 1999, I cleaned it out. Under the back seat was a canvas bag with some bills and gum wrappers on the top. I couldn't deal with it, so I put it in my office and purposely lost it. In 2006, I "found" it and went through it. At the bottom was a Whitman's 20-pound candy sampler box. I assumed it held photos and mementos from my late mother. Instead, there was a Sony "microcassette-corder" with thirty-two unlabeled cassettes he'd recorded. I was stunned. He was a prize-winning Union graduate, a decorated PT Boat commander, but couldn't use most mechanical appliances. The second cassette I played was the first he recorded. His opening made me transcribe every cassette.

He had a phenomenal mind and memory, astounding given his equally phenomenal drinking—apparent in parts of this. It took several years to transcribe and edit the tapes, some garbled from his haste or from heat damage. I removed most of the unrelated details and comments about the living. Periodically I used brackets to convey missing words or explain unspoken noises or actions. Otherwise, it is just as he spoke it, including the period slang and the Upper Hudson Valley regionalisms (e.g. *heighth* for height; *anyways* for anyway, etc.) he used to reveal his ultimate "jackpot"— his term for a huge crisis. He was in the midst of another one when he died; I was able to remove most references to it.

The "Kefauver Committee" he refers to was the 1950-51 "Special Committee to Investigate Organized Crime in Interstate Commerce" of US Senator Estes Kefauver. Kefauver's report dedicated a chapter on each major Organized Crime community, such as New York City, Chicago, or Los Angeles. And, then, there was Saratoga County, New York, where the Piping Rock was located. Saratoga's chapter had testimony from mobsters Meyer Lansky, Frank Costello, and Joe Adonis, who ran the Piping Rock, and from some of the Saratoga politicians and law enforcement officers who serviced the mob's activities.

To anyone upset by what he reveals, what can I say? We romanticize the past until we have to admit it. Saratoga loves romance and the past. The truth is sometimes another matter. My feeling is that his confession can't hurt him or the innocent family members and friends he mentions, now all dead—such as my mother, Martha Jane King ("Jane" or "Jennie"); his mother, Ann Fitzpatrick ("Annie"); or "Frank Sullivan," the *New Yorker* author and humorist, who was our Saratoga neighbor.

Finally, please be patient. It had to be difficult for him to record his truth aloud. He lingers on things and seems distracted. Alcohol does play a part, but far less than his obvious struggle to be truthful about something painful and dangerous. Above all, he was dying, another truth to face. Perhaps the best way to say it is to quote his own long standing advice as a pharmacist, given to customers and children alike: "Relax. Don't get your hemorrhoids in an uproar. It'll all come out in good time."

J. Cutshall-King

CHAPTER I

All right, let's get this underway. I'm George A. King. I'm dying and I need to confess what I know about the burning of the Piping Rock in Saratoga Springs in 1954. I know how it burned. I know why it burned . . . . I know I'm dying. Trust me. I've had this monkey on my back since 'fifty-four. Thonely . . . sorry . . . *the only* people I ever told were my wife, my second son. And I didn't tell them everything. I mean, about the Kefauver Committee . . . the mob, the others. Never even confessed it to a priest. Christ forgive me.

Only one other person ever knew it all. He burned the Piping Rock to the ground. I know he did . . . because, ah . . . because I was there. I need to tell you why. So, I'm letting this goddamn thing run and talking to it—to *you*. And *you* can listen. You can just *sit* there and *shut up* and *listen!* I'll tell it my way. I'm 68. I've got the Merck Manual by my bed. I did the diagnosis. Several diagnoses. I'm dying. Jiggly J. Joy. Dying of a myocardial infarction ten thousand miles from where I was *alive!* I was *alive* in the South Pacific! Sorry Jennie. It's supposed to be your marriage, I know. Sorry.

And now there's this fucking jackpot. Hope I'm dead before anyth . . . . [*Screeching noises; garbled speech. Voice resumes:*] Jesus! Screwed that up! Just let it run, George . . . unh . . . oh! God. My arm . . . pain . . . here. Get this under my tongue . . . . Unh, unh . . . 'Kay. Okay. Better. No more Manhattans, George? Just beer? Gotta ship to run . . . . Let me finish, God?

All right. About that night in Saratoga? I remember *everything*. Just like I do the war. Taking those boys outta the Amboina camps in 'forty-five. Broken glass shoved up their . . . their cocks. Us puking over the side. Fuckin' Japs. Same with Saratoga. I remember everything.

August sixteenth, nineteen fifty-four. I'm in my pharmacy, King's Pharmacy, in Fort Edward. George A. King, boy pharmacist, in the *Little Loser*. Ten years wasted in . . . .

Anyways, it was around nine-thirty. Streetlamps on. Chilly even for August. Still steaming in that store, though. Oh, *Jesus*, yes. I was in the back at the prescription table with a spatula compounding tablets from scratch. Just one light, over by the sink to keep bugs off the compound. Front of the store was dark, but I hadn't loc up . . . logged . . . shit! *Locked* up. Just in case some late night Lothario needed a Trojan. Good money in prophylactics in those pre-pill days, boys and girls. H'yock, h'yock! So, I was really absorbed in my work. Radio playin' "Make Love to Me." I always whistled it through my teeth, so I never heard him come in.

"*Hey, GEORGIE*! How's it goin' pops? Just whistle while you work, hey?" Jesus, he was bellowing! Outta reflex, I dropped back from the table. My hand went down by my side and knocked the spatula onto the floor. My heart was pounding in my ears. I was having a lot of nightmares then— jumping out of the rack, racing into the hallway, always on deck, always under fire. I shouted at him: "Jesus, you stupid bastard! You nearly . . . ."

"Nearly got shot?" he says. Laughed like a machine gun, big white Ipana grin. I'll remember that laugh if I live to a hundred. Which I won't. Anyway, he says, "Yeah, dad, saw the old hand-a-roo go down there. Old war reflexes never die, do they? Reet, Georgie? Hey, man, I know." I shot a look. He says *he* wasn't any slacker. Laughed that *stupid* laugh. I felt stupid, tried to cover it. He gave me a break, fussed with his porkpie hat—creased the front brim flat against the crown, shoved it back on his head. Looked like a kid in the movie magazines. Button down shirt, Argyle sweater. Snappy creased slacks, two-tone shoes. Buh-ruther.

"Harry . . ." I nearly said "Harry the Torch," which **no** one who ever knew him **ever** said to his face. Just did **not**. That's what **they** called him. Besides, not many people knew his nickname because they didn't know he was a torch. "You scared the *shit* out of me, Harry!" I barked at him and grabbed a clean spatula, started to mix again. "Why're you here, Harry? Getting ready to raid the high school dance? Stop in for a quick malted and a pack'a rubbers?"

Didn't faze him. "Slip me five, daddio," he says. What's *up*, I ask. "Nathan Shakin'," he says. Had all the lingo. He stood funny. Like a midshipman bracing for an officer. Shoulders *back*, chin *in*. Like this. Always moving, like somebody peeing on an electric fence. I said he looked like a tall Andy Hardy. He was close to my heighth, six-two. "Andy's old-timey, Georgie. Like that tune you're whistling? Really the *Tin Roof Blues*," he says. "Old-timey."

"Swell, a music lecture. And you're what, Harry? Twenty-eight?" He gets this funny look. Huh! What'd'I mean by *that*? Ooo. Hit a nerve. Good! The bastard. In Saratoga—when I ran MacFinn's Drug Store?—I got so friggin' sick of his perpetual boy routine. He says, whatever he is, he's *still* younger'n me, and laughs that laugh. Grrr. I told him, "Sure. You joined the

War right after ninth grade." Missing the War always got to these young hotshots.

"*Why* are you here, Harry?" Mr. Ants in His Pants is bouncing! I tell him to brace. He shrugs, says, "Jake with me, dad. Hey, get Fibber McGee on, huh? This crap's awful. Another minute'n it'll be Patti Page." I told him, leave it. He put his elbows on the countertop, fists on his face, a habit of his. One of those things to hide his face, I'm sure.

"*Why* are you *here*, Harry?" Goddamned if Patti Page didn't come on that very second and he gave me that, "*See?*" look and didn't answer me straight, but says, "Sheesh. Countertop high enough?" Christ! Since I first knew him in Saratoga in 'forty-seven, his mouth ran like a whippoorwill's ass in a windstorm. With me, anyways. He was a gem salesman. Supposed to be. I mean, he actually did that, but it was a cover. Knew his stuff, though.

I mixed, counting strokes as I talked. I'd had the countertop designed for my height so I didn't have to stoop. I was rolling the compound into a slender tube and he says, "Pills or tablets? Huh, Georgie? Pills or tablets?" I shush'im and cut the roll into thirty even tablets. He was like a little kid: "See? I remembered, didn't I? 'Pills are round and tablets are flat,' you'd always say in Saratoga. I remembered, didn't I, Georgie?"

"Yes, Lenny. Good job." Zoom! Right over his head. I cleaned up and set them to dry. It was a dying art. Goddamn pharmacy school grads now wouldn't know *how* to do that. I grabbed the towel and looked at him. I made my voice really flat, because I wanted him to know *I* wanted an answer. "*Why* are you *here*, Harry? *Why?*"

He'd been snapping his fingers and whistling one of those newer jazz tunes that aren't tunes and he stopped dead and looked at me. "Whaddya mean?" he says.

"It's not a difficult question. Brush-up course for pharmacy school? Try-outs for the school play?" I took out a Lucky out and lit up. "Why?" I didn't want him to see I was nervous.

He was moving up and down like the armature on an Oklahoma oil well. "Just dropped in. 'T's all." Voice was kind of uh, um—shit! What 'm' I saying? Whiney! Yeah. Whiney.

I remember looking at him. I'd walked back by the scales and he had the wall lamp to his back now, so his face was somewhat shadowed, but I could see his eyes. They were watching me. They did that in Saratoga—

when he was on a job. As God is my witness, they glowed. "You up here on a job, Harry? On a job in Fort Edward?"

His voice got very, uh . . . what? Mature. Strange for him. He tells me, "If I torched anything here, I'd torch the whole town for the good of humanity." For the good of humanity? *That* should have told me something. Then he says, "What are *you* doing here?" That caught me off guard, but I didn't get to answer 'cause he raced on, "Me? Just up to see my old friend . . . for good luck." Uh-huh.

"Puh-leeze. Give it a break, Harry." I can still smell the poplar trees and the Hudson blowing in through the window by the sink. And smell that Lucky. I can still *taste* that Lucky. Not a day goes by I don't want one. Wouldn't matter now. Sure wouldn't.

Yeah, well. Anyway he—I can't forget this—he laughed at me. Let's see. He says, "Gee-yor-gee. Come onnnn. Like a rabbit's foot, man. My good luck charm? Huh, man? Huh?" Always with the "Georgie" and "*man*" routine. Jesus. Well, I remind him it's been two years since I moved and I knew he wasn't out convalescing with Father Flanagan and the boys. More'n'a few places up and down the Hudson had gotten, shall we say, a tad above the flash point for wood? And in a style reminiscent of a style I knew? His eye gave that twitch I knew. I said, "You've been two-timing me, Harry. Yeah, a girl can tell." I remember my heart pounding in my ears and asking him if he needed a little something to calm him, maybe a Seconal, Nembutal. I asked him very slowly, really watching my words. Never saw him blow, but I'd heard. Who knew? I always had an unmarked bottle ready for my regulars and I reached for it.

"Aw, Georgie, I don't do that stuff. I've always told you that." Surprising. He seemed genuinely offended. "Just don't do it. Ixnay on the ope-day, Georgie."

The "Georgie" bit was really grating on my nerves. Christ, how many times had I told him I hated it? And that whiney weird accent. Sounded like New York. I told'im he seemed to be doing okay without me, seemed to be getting his luck elsewhere. I made a limp wrist and said, "You left me for another. I'm wounded." His looked like he'd been on bennies for a week. Not his face, I mean how he never stopped moving. I was gettin' a little antsy myself. I needed to get across the street to the Manhattan bar, have a few before bedtime. Jennie'd just had our fourth in May and, uh . . . wasn't doing well. Rough birth. Unexpected. Couldn't afford it. God forgive me, we'd planned the others. I told the priest, "I'm not killing *my* wife for a passel of kids I can't feed." I'll probably go to hell. And for selling a million prophylactics, too. Jesus. That'd be the least of it.

Okay, okay, so, um, so I'm trying to figure out how to get rid of him and I say, "Hey, good to see you Harry," and he picks it up the hint and puts his hands up and flaps 'em like he's stopping traffic. "Wait wait wait wait wait... Okay, Georgie..."

"*George.*" I had my teeth clenched.

"Reet, dad. *George.* Reet." All this hepcat talk. "I came 'cause I needed those *special* wrapping papers only *you* can sell me." He winks. "Need to 'wrap something up'?" He's making quotation marks with his fingers and he's moving his hands like somebody directing a plane down a runway. Got his face turned slightly to one side and he's shaking his head "yes" with this "come on" smile. Jesus. Looked like a kid practicing to get laid for the first time.

And me? I'm bug-eyed. "Jesus!" I yell at 'im, "You're up *here* to buy wrapping paper? *Here?* You can't get cellophane and scotch tape in Saratoga?" Or wherever the hell he was before. I always knew when something was going to get *warm* between Saratoga and Manhattan. Harry'd appear at MacFinn's and, bang! Buy every box of cellophane wrapping paper and scotch tape we had. He'd wrap the places in it. Cellulose fiber? Not a trace. I always had cartons of it because of him. "You had to come *here?*" I was mystified. I was an idiot!

"Sure! Hey-hey! Course I did!" Ugh! That bizarre way of speaking of his! I said it was stupid. He could buy 'em wholesale. "Lookit who's being stoopid," he says. You could always hear New York in his voice when he was excited or angry. "I can nevah buy it that way. I'm not a business. What's somebody gonna say if I buy cases that way? Huh?" I can't imitate his accent, but you get it. Boy, he was dancing. Then suddenly, like his strings were cut, he relaxed and says he *always knows* Georgie has what he needs. Old habit on my part, I guess, but, goddamnit, I did have cartons of it out back. Still, stupid me, I thought he was full of shit and told him so.

"Cool, daddio. You're hip. Lookit. I gotta get a little '*something*' done— in Saratoga? Can't go in MacFinn's the way I used to. You know? To *buy* it? Like when you were there?" He let out this big sigh, like he was my mother's age. I thought I'd start to laugh for a second. "It's not the same place anymore, George." He sighed again. "Just not the same Saratoga anymore."

Certainly wasn't, which was precisely why *I* wasn't there anymore, but I wasn't going to say *that* to *him*. Jesus no! Instead I said, "Relax. Don't get your hemorrhoids in an uproar." I was only too happy to sell it. The lad always paid a lot. I needed it. But I didn't need him around. No.

He beamed this big grin and said, "Where they at, Jah-gee?"

The Georgie bit. I pointed to the back beyond the prescription room, told him he'd see it by the table where I cut glass. The bastard said, "Pops! You cut glass, too? What a man!" And he made this limp wrist, pursed his lips in a kiss and winked.

"And sell paint, perfume, garden seeds, douche bags, rubbers and drugs—moron," I told him. "It's what small pharmacies in small towns do."

"Reet, man." And I will always remember him saying, "What the hell **are** you doing here, George? There's Nathan Shakin' here." I was trying not to ask myself that same thing—and I didn't want *him* asking me. *God*, he was really on my frigging nerves. I said something like, oh, I wanted to own my own store, lot of nice people here, etcetera.

"Lotta nice people everywhere, dad. But here? I mean, long on nuthin' and short on somethin'—a drag, man." He kept snapping the brim of his hat—really getting on my frigging nerves. I said that, didn't I? Anyway, I sent 'im out back pronto 'cause I had to hit the head. Normally you can set a clock by my bowel movements or taking a leak, but I suddenly had to pee. Case of nerves. So, I'm coming out of the crapper as Harry gets back and he says, "That the head, Georgie?" I said, no, it was a confessional. I just got absolution. That cracked him up. Who ever knew what would'r wouldn't? He looks at it and says, *"That's* weird."

Lemme explain this. The head was on the landing of a closed off stairway that had gone to the second floor. The landlord had made an apartment up there and we lived over the store four years. Jane, ah, Jane got really depressed. Feingold said, buy her a house. Her dream. Never mine, frankly. I'd grown up in a boarding house. I was on stateside leave in January 'forty-five. Laid over in San Francisco'n won eight hundred iron men in a crap game at the Drake Hotel. Bought her a fur coat. She said, "We could've had that for a down payment on a house." I guess I never really understood those kinds of things. I think I disappointed her a lot.

Well, anyways, Harry stepped up into the crapper, laughed and said, "A throne fit for George King, hey dad?" I was sick of his "dad" and "daddio" crap. A bitch of a day and then he shows up. I didn't need a return to all that. I needed a touch of Dr. Budweiser's medicinal wonder. I went out front to make sure I'd turned off the hot fudge machine and the nut roaster. That's when I heard the crash. I ran back like a jackrabbit—I could still really move then, like when I was playing ball. He was on the floor. I saw blood. He was clutching his arm and groaning, saying he'd missed the steps. I was afraid he'd wake up Jennie and shushed him. "Can you get up?" I whispered. Yes. Was he dizzy, hit his head? Not that he knew of. I treated his cut. He laughed that insipid machine gun laugh. "You a doctor?" I said I was going to be one, but I got back from the war and, well . . . . That's life.

"I know," he said seriously. I laughed at him. What'd he know about life. "More'n you know," he says. He was clutching his right arm up by his shoulder and wincing and I got him into the captain's chair by the old safe, got a better light on, checked his pupils. Nothing. I wasn't sure where the cut came from. It wasn't serious, but he had a helluva a lump on his shoulder. I brought back some ice from the soda fountain and packed his shoulder. I was surprised at how it was already coloring, which didn't seem natural. "You have blood problems?" He gives this blank look. "Blood problems in your family?" Yes. His uncle died from it at forty-eight.

I thought about how, here I was, thirty-five and scared to death of turning forty, because my father had died at thirty-four. To me, I was so old. And now I'm gonna die and I can't get over how young I am. *Sixty-eight!* How's that right, God? And Jane? Dead at sixty-five? *God!* Answer me! How's that *right?* How . . . ?

Phew! Phew boy! Sorry! Man, I'm sorry. Don't mean to cry. Doing a lot of that lately, like some old man. All right, where was I? He has this bump. . . blood prob . . . . All right, I remember. I remember. He was looking at me and saying, "What?"

And—listen to this. This is how insane it was getting. I said to him, "What?"

And he said, "*What?*"

And I said, "*WHAT* what?" Christ, Abbott and Costello.

He whispers, "You said 'Forty,' dad.' Okay?"

Son of a bitch's hearing was like mine, sharp. I told him I was thinking of a page number from the Merck manual. "Check. Am I gonna die, pops?" He used that word pops fi. . . .

[The tape ran out here. The next tape starts with him saying, "I don't know if this is working," but he obviously hit the rewind button by mistake and something further was lost.]

"....arge. Go on. One for the road. A parting gift. Go ahead. I gotta close up." I heard him leave. I get ready to go, thinking about Saratoga and the old times when Harry used to come in to buy cellophane. Sometimes he'd buy a couple of thousand dollars worth of expensive perfumes, watches. Expensive tastes. Expensive times. Times I wanted to forget.

It's, oh, not even five minutes later. I'm in the back'n'hear the front door and call out, "Hey! Closed up. You want a six-inch swimsuit, come back tomorrow," figuring somebody wants rubbers. No noise and I think, oh great, it's a woman'n I offended her.

Instead, there's a panting voice, like a man overboard in rough seas: "Georgie. George!" I ran down that left aisle to him by the time he hit the cases with the perfumes and colognes. I remember hissing at him, "What're'you doin' back here?"

"I got trouble, George—trouble moving my arm!" He's clutching it like it's going to fall off. I guess I'm not saying anything and he says, "Armus no movus?" and then suddenly he says in this high-pitched voice, all serious and scared, "I can barely open my car door. I don't think I can shift gears to drive!" I didn't know what to say. I *wanted* to say tough shit, but just mumbled something and he tries to put both arms up, you know, so's to put his hands on both my shoulders, but winces with the pain. "Georgie! Georgie, I'm in trouble if I can't do this, George!" He's begging. I can hear his voice. I can always hear his voice. I've heard it playing inside my skull for years. It's whining, "I'm in real trouble—spent my advance! A lotta bread, lotta iron men. It's big. **It's big!** I can't pay it back!" Now he's prancing around clutching his arm and shouting, "How do I tell you this? It's not *just* the money. *Christ*, dad, it's big. I'm in it. Oh, God, I'm in it." All these years. I can hear him like a minute ago.

I say something like, why doesn't he get somebody else? I swear the bastard starts to cry. Breath in short little gasps. "Nobody's supposed to do this, except me," he's saying, "nobody's supposed to know except me." He grabs me. "I *have* to do like they told me to."

I felt . . . I, I didn't want any part of this. I didn't reply and he screams, "Don't you *get* it? *Nobody's* supposed to do this, except *me*. If they hire somebody else, they'll *kill* me." I told him to keep it down. He's gasping but laughing—that kind of laugh guys make when they're tryna keep it light but are ready to soil themselves?

Still, oh, I don't know, though. It still seemed like he was full of shit. I mean, these frigging younger guys could be so melodramatic, especially if they hadn't seen active duty. We were by the perfume testers, Matchabelli fragrances floating in the air. I said, "*Come on*, Harry."

And he cuts me off with a whisper like a bullet . . . hissing like those snakes in the Philippines: "*They* will *kill* me. It has to be done the way *they* want it."

Let me say this. You have to know when men are telling you something true because they are afraid of dying. I'd known it before. I knew it now. I said in this very low, controlled voice, "What are you talking about, Harry? Who're you working for?" He shook his head no. I tried angry: "I asked you *what* the hell you're talking about. *Who's* this `they' you're working for?"

He was shaking his head "no" again and saying softly, "They will *kill* me." Now I was *really* pissed off. "For **Christ's sakes**, if you can't tell me who, tell me what this *job* is! *Tell me!*" I'm screaming at him now. It was Saratoga all over again. That same *crap* all over again. I could smell it, like the perfume and the cologne. "*Tell me!*"

He picked up a tester bottle and smelled it. And then in this almost far away voice, he said to the bottle, "It's Piping Rock, George. They want me to torch the Piping Rock."

CHAPTER 2

Well, there was this long, just incredibly long silence. He never moved. I never moved. We sold all sorts of fine traveling clocks and you could hear the ones that customers would wind up, just ticking away. I don't remember one car going by. I don't know how long we stood there, you know, without saying anything. It was so hard to grasp. Finally I said, really, really low, "Christ Jesus, Harry. You've been hired to torch Piping Rock? *The* Piping Rock Casino, Harry?" My head was so clear, not another thought in my mind. I whispered, "Is that right?"

His head went up and down. I thought he was going to keel over. God, I was thinking to myself, it's starting all over again. Anyway, I got him over by the counter away from the front door, got some more ice from the fountain. The iceman still delivered for the Coke machine and there was still a pretty good-sized block. I chipped off a chunk with the ice pick, wrapped it in a towel and put it on his neck and shoulder.

He smiled. "The iceman cometh, hey?"

"The iceman broughteth this chunk in a towel. Can you hold it?" He nodded yes and I brought him back a soda and something for the pain. "Take these," I told'im. "They'll ease the pain." He shook his head no. "Go on. It's not dope. You won't get hopped up."

The bastard corrected me: "High, Georgie, high," and smiled. I felt a friggin' hundred.

He took it. I tried to make sense of it. Swell. Why'd he have to tell me he's going to be doing the Cocoanut Grove without customers? It was quiet and I didn't know what to say so I said I'd heard the place was empty. He didn't say anything or make any movement. "I mean, who wants this?" I ask him. "The owner?"

He started to say, "He doesn't know anything . . ." and then stopped dead and screamed in that hissing voice again, "I can't tell yah that, fa'Chrisssake! *You're tryna get me killed!*" That accent again.

He drains the soda and, suddenly—bang!—he's up and moving around again. *Boom!* Like a jack-in-the-box! On the balls of his feet, still clutching his arm. "Crazy, man. I can't move it, pops. What am I going to do? Huh? Huh? What? I gotta get down there!" He starts to hit it, smack it and I tell him to stop. "I have *got* to get down there!" Some traffic passed out front. I was afraid someone would see us or Jane would come down.

I got him to stop batting at it and asked him if he could move it any better. He said it again, he couldn't drive. Without thinking, I said I couldn't drive for him, if that's what he meant. My store was dark and the lights from the Manhattan—that was a bar across the street. Did I say that? Um, well, the store had huge plate glass windows and the Manhattan's lights lit up his whole body, moving up and down like a piston.

Then he suddenly stops dead, whirls around, and stares at me. I watch him. He says, "Why not?"

"Why not what?" I ask. Jesus! I knew what he meant and I didn't want to think that *that* was what he meant. What I wanted was a quiet beer, not all this. Christ, here's this torch in my store buying me out of cellophane and scotch tape and all I want is for him to be gone. *Gone!* You understand? I kept thinking over and over, "My God. Torching the Piping Rock." I could see the place, smell it again. Hell, Jennie and I'd been in there enough, seen the acts, the gambling. Then there was the money from it and MacFinn's and . . . I didn't want that again.

He had stopped bouncing and he's saying, over and over. "Drive for me! Drive for me!"

"*Drive?* For *you?*"

"Hey-hey? Yeah!" he says. Weird. "Hey-hey? Right-right!"

"Right-right, my ass," I yell to him. "You out on a Section 8, Harry? You nuts?" You won't believe this. We were by the Kemp's nuts display case where we had all these roasted peanuts and cashews and I reached in and grabbed a handful and gave him a handful. They were still warm. With a mouthful of nuts he asks, "why not? He had that Andy Hardy look on again and Andy and Judy were going solve it all with a big fire in the barn.

I tried to calm my voice like I did onboard in a crisis. *Brother*, I wasn't calm inside. I *told* him I couldn't get involved—didn't have anything to do with me. Certainly didn't. I was pacing, trying to keep my voice low, trying not to attract any attention from the troops out on the street.

I said, I don't know, something like I didn't really know him well enough to do that. He says to me: "I've known you since nineteen forty-seven."

"Swell," I say. "We're blood brothers." I lit up a smoke, paced, and then went back to him. "I can't. I just can't. That's all." Honestly? I was scared shitless. He starts in. It's just this once, just this once. I said, "I've got a store. Look around," I said. *That* was a major mistake. He rolled his eyes. I hadn't seen a look that sarcastic since 'forty-five, when I told Jane I wanted to re-enlist. She threw a baby carriage at me down a full flight of stairs. "Okay, so it's not MacFinn's, but it's *my* store." Nothing. So I tried, "I have a family. I couldn't get involved in all that, could I?"

You know what that little shithead said? "You mean 'again,' don't you?"

I was pissed off this time—I shot back at 'im that I *never* did anything like that! I just sold him the fucking cellophane and scotch tape. That's all. I was really bitching and he cuts me off, "All right, all right, all right!" he *snaps* at me. "You weren't a friggin' Boy Scout, Georgie. All that take-money in the cellar of MacFinn's every night? People getting their 'necessities' from you. You *knew* why I came in to buy that. Jim Leary knew."

Okay, so he was right. But I reminded him *I* didn't bring the money over from the Piping Rock and I didn't count it and I didn't take it away. Okay? And if I always had more cellophane and scotch tape than we needed? Well, that was because Uncle Jim *told* me to. I *also* reminded him I didn't work for Jim Leary anymore. Uncle Jim may own MacFinn's, I said, but he doesn't own King's Pharmacy and he doesn't own me.

Harry walked toward me. He's all Mr. Smooth, all "this isn't about MacFinn's or Leary" and jerking his head this way and making his eyes go back and forth, like somebody's shooting his best side. Reminded me of Dex Seton, a pimple-faced little creep who always pretended he was more connected than he was. He spent the season acting like he owned Broadway. Dex did that same thing with his eyes. Made you wanta puke.

I went quiet. Harry got panicky. "Listen. Listen, I'm willing to pay you. No! I'm *gonna* pay you —two fifty for the ride down and back." Oh, *baby*! You have to understand. That was a pile in those days—a *lot* of berries. I kept saying no. I can still hear him screaming: "Five hundred. *Five hundred!*" He was at me like a, like a carnie. "Five…***NO! NO!*** A thousand! A thousand clams! A *thousand* iron men! I'll give you a ***THOUSAND*** *fucking dollars!*"

Auuugh. Damn! I can't tell you . . . I was just . . . flabbergasted . . . flabbergasted. A thousand bucks. Boys and girls, that *is* a *lot* of berries. Like ten now, oh, hell, more. You could get an Olds for that in 'fifty-four. And I, I really was just so desperate at that stage. I think the little bastard felt he had me. I'd started fairly well capitalized and then came the business with . . . . Well, it doesn't matter. I said, "Let's go across the street and have a drink. Talk it over."

He pointed to the Manhattan and laughed this, this, really filthy laugh, like he's gagging. "There? *Me?* Drink in *that* lousy gin joint? Bernard Baruch drink there? Joe DiMaggio? Joe Adonis?" Funny. I should've picked up on that, but I, well, my mind was on the money. "Get a grip, pops," he says. I should've slapped his mouth. Besides, he can't have anyone seeing him in town. He started bouncing again. "Come on, Georgie. If you need one, we'll getcha a drink on the way. Hey-hey! With a grand, you can buy me one. A grand, George."

A grand! What was I thinking? Jesus, listen to me. What was I thinking? I *wasn't* thinking! I wasn't thinking straight when I said, "How long would it be?" I feel he thought he had me, because he started detailing what he had to do and so on. I said we'd take my car and he shot back, "That Sunday-go-to-picnic heap? Like hell, daddio! I got mine souped, got my tools in it, plus an extra gas tank. Does a hundred and thirty. Think you can drive something like that?"

I whistled and asked what it was.

"Studebaker Commodore, pops." Same car I had in Saratoga.

The bastard knew he had me.

I wasn't thinking, I know. Was it just the money? I don't know. I just wasn't thinking. But the bastard knew he had me.

CHAPTER 3

He said he had the car near the river by the yacht basin. I'd hoped it wasn't too near. But at least he'd had the brains not to park in back of the building next door. The Whalen brothers usually sat out on the second floor back porch with their drinking menagerie. They'd be watching every move. Be okay if I went down. I belonged there.

I don't know if I belonged there, but I ended up there.

I told him we should go separately, not to draw attention. I needed to go up and tell my wife I was going to be a while. He agreed and shot down the next alley by the A&P. I went across the street for a beer.

Before he'd even arrived, I'd already been upstairs to check on Jane. She was asleep, the three older kids and the baby, too, thankfully. She needed a lot more sleep than I ever did. I worried about her after this pregnancy. Didn't want her ending up doing what her mother did, going down to the river for the long swim.

The Manhattan was pretty well filled, the long bar on the left and the booths on the right. I haven't smoked in ten years and I can still smell that air, filled with beer and cigarettes, heat, sex. It was dark. The smoke made it darker. I was sorry I'd come.

I went to leave when Abe called out from behind the bar, asked how I was. Shit, I thought, I'm here, so I'd better order something. He could barely hear me 'cause the jukebox was cranked up so loud and everybody kept coming up to bitch that somebody was playing "Heart of My Heart" over'n'over. It was so **big** that year. I remember it so well. "Too bad we had to parrrrt. I *know* a tear would glisten, if once more I could listen, to that gang that sang heart of my h . . . ." Oh, Jesus, my chest hurts. Glad nobody can hear me carry on like this.

Anyways, I'm asking Abe for a sandwich and some beers to go when this whiney voice starts bitching that somebody'd filled the jukebox with nickels —"put *another* nickel in, to the nickelodeon…" Hey, I can't even sing anymore without my chest hurting . . . Anyways, like I said, somebody kept playing "Heart of My Heart" over'n'over and everybody's bitching. I'd told Abe I'm only in for a couple of beers to go'n Abe'd given me that look that says he's not supposed to, but then I slipped him a few bob and, *mirabile dictu*, the planets do not fall from their appointed rounds and life goes on.

The usual cast of regulars was there. Holdovers from the seven to three who'd been there so long their asses had grafted to the stools. And young guys taking the edge off with cheap beers here before they headed out to chase tail in Lake George. I was thirty-five and they made me feel a hundred. Jesus. I'm almost twice that now.

I'm dying for Abe to shake a leg. I didn't want Mr.-Ants-in-His-Pants to come over, 'cause this was a small town and everyone'd be asking questions. I scanned the booths and saw Willie—Willimena. Already gone. She always sat slightly hunched over, clutching a Camel, scrawny, eyes all sunken in. She had the "curse of the Irish." She was Black Irish—had straight black hair she wore in a ponytail. Her husband, Will, was with her. Will'n'Willie, they called them. "Will-he-or-won't-he?" they'd say. Their little boy, Stevie, sat between'em. Poor little shit— head lolling around, eyes rolling in their sockets. He couldn't speak at all. He waved. I winked at him and shot him a big grin. He beamed all over. Alcohol . . . .

Abe was handing me a brown paper bag and had the beers wrapped in his *Daily Mirror* so they wouldn't clink. Somebody in back of me was saying, "She was just beautiful once, like Jinx Falkenburgh. Hardta believe I know. Abe can tell you." I slipped Abe a wad of bills and left that guy still talking about her. The first Willimena I ever saw, I was a kid delivering papers at Betty Redtops in Mechanicville. I've seen them everywhere, ever since. Twenty years can kill you.

Normally I'd hit the Manhattan, have a dozen beers and all's well with the world. But that night my teeth were on edge. I crossed Broadway toward my store, angrier with Harry with every step. Here I was getting ready to drive a torch to the Piping Rock—letting myself get dragged back into that whole . . . whole mess again.

Hang on a minute. Ahhh. That's good. Dee-LISH. Thank you, Dr. Budweiser! Okay. So, I walked down the alleyway between the Little Loser and the Whalen brother's building and he says in this stage whisper you could've heard in China, "Georgie, baby. Where the hell you been?" It lifted me out of my shoes. God, I was jumpy! I whispered back to him to shut the fuck up until we got to the car. I pointed up to the second floor. "My family? Up there?" And pointed up to the building next door. "You think anyone saw you?"

He hisses—I'll never forget this—he hisses, "What do you think I do for a living? Run a jackhammer? My job's get in, get it done and get out—

unheard and unseen. " The punk repeated "unheard and unseen" a million times until I told him that that's what he should do right now. We looked along the length of big wooden porches off the back of the Whalen brothers' old brick building. The brothers and their drunken buddies weren't there. All quiet on the Western Front. We snuck past a trailer and a shack, but it didn't matter. They were just old men, all dead drunk.

His car was near the quay wall and, like I said, thankfully not too close to the yachts. But, they were dark. Neither one of us were smoking. It was just understood. I could smell the river. If you've ever worked on the Hudson, you know its smell. There's this line about rivers, can't think of where I heard it, but it goes, "thrilling sweet and rotten, unforgettable unforgotten." I'll always know that smell. I worked on the dredges on the Hudson, the Mohawk and Great Lakes. Should have stayed on them—or at least in the Navy. I was a man there.

So . . . ? So what? Oh . . . okay. I heard keys jingle and heard'im say "Catch. . . ." Or start to anyway. Instead he makes a gurgling noise and clutches his arm and drops'em. I picked'em up. Fool. Throwing me keys in the dark. I had great hands, but if he hadn't dropped'em, the sons-a-bitches would have sailed right over the quay wall. I tried to ask if he'd broken his arm, but he put me off and asked if I know how to drive it. Really sarcastically. Drive it? Drive that peach? A big 'fifty-one Studebaker Commodore? You bet I did.

I turned the key and it purred. It had a huge engine in it, but it was as quiet as an electric train. It was like the one I had except that it had weight, I mean *weight*. He had a stick on the floor instead of the steering column, which was odd. We slid out with the lights off. I think it was somewhere after ten, but it was summer, people were out, so I told him we needed to avoid coming out on Broadway. I snaked through some back alleys until it was okay to turn on the lights. I'd decided I'd drive a mile and talk him out of it. Or at least get out and walk home. This was, well, just insane. And definitely not my business. *Definitely* not anymore.

He fiddled with the radio dials 'n bitched that he couldn't get "The Shadow." I remember when I said it was the wrong night, that sent 'im off. Oh, yeah, he forgot, on last night, damn, hated to miss it, blah, blah, blah. He kept saying, "Who knows what evil lurks in the hearts of men?" He was telling me to pull over somewhere so he could show where everything was in the car and meanwhile was blabbering on about how he had followed "The Shadow" from the start, but liked Orson Wells best. Blah, blah, blah.

After a couple of miles, I stopped where we wouldn't be seen, near Lock 5 on the canal. He was like a kid, showing off all these custom built, hidden drawers. Anything a cop could see looked like part of his jewelry business. I had opened this silver polish bottle and he told me to be careful. I sniffed it and said, "Lighter fluid?" He did admit even he needed a really fast start sometimes, but he bragged that nobody ever picked up a trace. He was right, you know. When Harry the Torch lit a manse, ashes and embers were his only calling card.

"Heart of My Heart" came on the radio and I started to sing with it: "Heart of my heart, how I love that melody . . . ." Suddenly he stopped everything, as if he'd seen a cop.

"What's up?" I asked. He looked at me like I was, well, I don't how to say this, but, as if, as if I were dead. It shook me. You have to understand. I wasn't *that* long out of the service. Nine years was nothing after what we went through. "What's eating you"? I said.

"What the hell you singing *that* for?"

"What's wrong with it?" He mumbled something about bad memories. "Of what, Harry? Snookie Lanson murdering it on The Hit Parade?" A pretty snappy rejoinder, I thought. He gives me a weepy wailer about this dolly at Skidmore, their favorite song, they went too far, she left him—you know. And I was—shall we say?—a little less than sensitive? I said, something like, oh, what a tearjerker. Sell it to a washboard weeper or write Dear Abby, 'cause slap'n'tickle regret stories did nothing for me. That snapped him out of it! Told me to fuck myself. H'yock! H'yock! I had all the hand holding I could take as a skipper—didn't do a hell of a lot of it there, usually just for a Dear John letter. I don't deal well with all this emotion, um, introspection. It's not natural. You just do what you need to do, don't think about it and get on with life.

He went to take a leak. I opened the beers, drank one, and started on the sandwich. When he got back in the car, he was over it and that was fine with me. He didn't want any of the beer or sandwich. The mosquitoes were horrible and I had to get this over. I've hated heat'n'bugs'n'rain since the war. In the Philippines, you thought you'd rot. Anyways, he wanted to know when we were shoving off and I popped it on him. Said it was nuts.

Said I couldn't be an arsonist's chauffer. I rather liked that phrase—an arsonist's chauffer.

He went ape shit—blew high, wide and handsome, like he was on bennies. Up and down, out of the car, back in the car, lighting a cigarette and throwing it away, lighting another, wringing his hands, and grunting and wincing while he does it, and all the time his mouth going like a whippoorwill's ass in a windstorm. "What's it, the money? Huh? The money?" I denied it, but he kept at me, "You need more? Huh? HUH?" He's up against the wall, he says. They're gonna kill him—whoever *they* are. Whatever I want, let's talk about it. The whole nine yards.

I told him I wanted—shit, *wanted?*—I told him I *needed* the original grand he offered, but this thing was *nuts!* I said it took me two years to extract my life from Saratoga and then, suddenly—bang!—here it is, back again, the Ghost of Saratoga Past.

He popped open a side panel that you couldn't even have seen on the door, which was open, and in the light from overhead I saw he had a pistol. It was small, looked like a .22 with inlay on the handle. "Oh Christ," I'm thinking, "The bastard's going to shoot me."

Instead, he hands it to me, butt end first, and says—tears in his eyes, but very calmly—"Here, man. Take it. Blow my head off." He is deadpan, not an emotion in his voice. "Go ahead, Georgie. Go on, man." He was really starting to scare me.

"Oh, come on, Harry." I was like a, like a skipper to a new seaman who's scared, trying to shame him out of it. I laughed, "Wherejah get this? A Crackerjacks box?" He takes the pistol in his left hand and cocks it awkwardly, 'cause his right arm's obviously killing him, 'n puts the barrel to his temple.

Without thinking—I can't believe I did this—but I snatched it from him, stepped out of the car and threw it in the canal. All in a second! Oh, he starts wailing, crying about it being "Grandmother's pistol." I threatened to punch him in his bad arm and he shut up. Then, suddenly, *very, very* calmly he says, "Five big. Five thousand." And then he pauses. And then he says, "But you'll help me tape the place."

I'd already figured that out before "five thousand" had left his mouth. God forgive me, the bastard knew he had me. I figured, "Oh, well, in for a dime, in for a dollar." Five thousand, actually.

CHAPTER 4

Now I'm in for the next surprise. I headed south on Route 4 for Schuylerville, while he was fiddling with the radio. He was getting signals from all over eastern North America and kept twiddling with the dial. "Jesus. Settle on something!" I yelled and he when looked up, he screamed that I had to turn around.

"I don't understand." The car, he says. Turn the car around. I say he's not making sense. I figured we'd go over 29, through Schuylerville, and then just before Saratoga, turn down Gilbert to the Piping Rock. He shouted we hadta go back over 197 to 9—he's got to go to some place on Route 9. Why didn't I see it right then? Jesus, hindsight's twenty-twenty.

I ask if he intends to drive into Saratoga on Route 9. You know, it's still the season. Lots of people are there to see the ponies. I'm making like I'm on ship to shore, "State troopers. Over. George and Harry here, coming down on Route 9, on our way to torch the Piping Rock. Can we get an escort? Over." And he makes this turn around motion with his left hand and gets this Father Time voice on. "Listen, I have every inch of this planned. I know *what* I have to do and *why*." *He* doesn't plan things to get caught and *he* hasn't been caught yet. And then he leans over as best he can and screams at my ear, *"Turn the fucking car around!"*

I jammed on those brakes, whipped that wheel hard, did a U-turn in the middle of 4 and then punched the gas hard to pull it out of it. I heard him hit the door on his bad side, but he never yelled—just asked if I'd messed my skivvies. I admitted I thought the car'd tip over. He said it couldn't've. He had fifty pound bars of lead bolted on the undercarriage and a V-8 that could haul a DE.

He's back screwing with the dial again and I was trying to ask him where he had all that body work done, but right at that moment he landed on a station with big band music and hollered, "Oh, yeah! Teddy Wilson."

"So, who did it?" He looks at me and says—in the same breath, "Attleboro. My grandfather. Aw, man. That's Goodman's thirty-eight concert at Carnegie Hall."

I said, "Your grandfather from Brooklyn?"

He isn't really listening to me, 'cause he's pounding the beat with one hand on the dash. "No," he says, "my grandfather's from Attleboro, Massachusetts. Oh, yeah, go Teddy! It was cold outside Carnegie Hall that night, man." And then, wham! He flipped it to another station with bebop and he's bobbing his head to the squeak'n'squawk crap, and saying it had the groove and all that. And he turned it up. Natch. Which pissed me off and I screamed for him to leave it, because I like Benny Goodman, but he shouts that it's too late and too old timey, like Beethoven. He pointed to the radio. "This is The Bird." Whoever the hell that was. He snapped his fingers. My kids' rock and roll made more sense than that crap.

We'd crept back through Fort Edward and were out on 197, when I asked him where to. With the radio blasting, it sounded like he said, "Put the dog in." I asked him again and he screamed, "The Brown Log Inn!" I turned the goddamn radio'n squeak'n'squawk off. I was nervous enough without that. "Get your friggin' hearing aids fixed, pops!"

I ignored that and asked him why the Brown Log Inn? See, the Brown Log was a locals bar—a country western place filled with shitkickers. He needed to see this dolly. I said, "Oh, swell! You're gonna play slap and tickle with Ma'n'Pa Kettle's daughter while we're doing *this*?" And suddenly he was really dry and unemotional, patiently explaining everything as if I were an idiot, like my old biology prof at Union, who very unsentimentally described kissing as sucking on a fifty-six foot tube of shit.

Junior explained he had lined up a client at the Brown Log Inn. She wouldn't know it, but she'd providing him with an alibi. He'd see her before he went and then right after. "I always do this. With those delayed fuses I designed, I can tell you to the minute when they end. And after, I'll be with her the entire time they're doing what they're supposed to."

If I hadn't been so stunned, I would have asked him where the hell I was supposed to be during the post-bonfire period, but all I remember saying was, "You have a client? At the Brown Log Inn?" It was not clicking. I told him I thought he just sold jewelry to stores. No, he's got individual clients, including a couple Skiddies he sells to. This is one.

Ohhh . . . . Now it was making sense. Skidmore College girls always went the Brown Log. I guess for them it was slumming. Most of them had money, I mean *real* money. Old, new, it didn't matter. Annie was a Skidmore housemother at the Spring Street House at this point. She'd bring Jane boxes of silk underwear, dresses, fur stoles the girls just left behind at the end of the year. Still in wrapping paper and string from Bergdor . . . .

[*There was a clicking and some other noise; apparently he had accidently hit the wrong button. It's difficult to reconstruct what came before, but here they are talking about the woman he is to meet.*]

"Nah, Jah-gee."

The Georgie bit again.

"I'm not hillbilly enough for her. But she never saw me the way I really grew up." He said he had this image.

I laughed at him, but he was too entranced with his own story and kept flipping the cap of the Zippo on and off. I borrowed it to light a Lucky. I recognized the emblem just from the feel. He just blabbed right on. "She likes buying finished stones, no settings, just loose. Gets her jollies outta keeping them loose in her pocket and fondling her jewels." He made a lewd remark about fondling his and said, "She thinks she's the cat's meow. But she doesn't know anything, especially about that dolly she pals around with. Yes, she's somethin' else. She likes black meat."

I was thinking about his "cat's meow" remark when that registered. I have to admit I was shocked. He never noticed. "Guess she likes to ask, `How far is the Old Brown Log Inn?'" He laughed at that one until he coughed. "How would you know?" I asked him. It sounded concocted. Well, he always went to Congress Street, had somebody cook him a meal, bathe him. "Etcetera," he added. I knew etcetera.

"I see her girlfriend down there a lot. Comes late at night—both ways?" He said she dressed like a slut and banged any colored guy she could find. Apparently liked an audience, too. He was there one night watching this act where this Negro—he always said "Negro"—woman goes right down on the floor in a split and, shall we say, *snatches* a quarter up off the floor? Sucks that coin right up off the floor. "Believe it or not," Harry said.

Which made me think it was something Mr. Ripley wouldn't feature in the Sunday comics. Anyway, where was I . . . ? Oh. So, one night hotshot was there and the colored gal did her trick and Miss Skiddie boomed out, "*I can do that*" in this snotty voice and I guess everybody just *gasped*. Harry got laughing so hard and he says, "So the Negro gal gets really, really sassy and says, 'You couldn't pick up the clap with that tah-nee whahte pussy a'yoh-wuz.'"

I think the colored girl had something on, but, in a flash, the Skiddie is up there wearing nothing but a smile—and down she goes. Harry said, "Oh man, Georgie, she was built! The combo starts playing, just like they do for the other woman and, by Jesus, Miss Skiddie did it. At that point Major Bowes announced she won the contest! **Sha-*zamm***, baby! I think they actually became friends after that."

He went quiet. I wish he'd kept on talking. I was collecting my thoughts, the last thing you want to do when you're hurtling down the road to burn down a casino. You want distraction. I was scared. How were we going to get in and out, do everything we needed to do, not be seen? And, worse, things weren't making sense. Why were these Skiddies back in Saratoga during the summer? College wasn't in session till September. I was rattled. I shouldn't've been so rattled.

We were zooming, his blond head bobbing, fingers snapping to his goddamn bebop when, thank God, a *Gunsmoke* commercial interrupted. It made me remember his pistol. I apologized for tossing it in the canal.

"I'll get another," he says, "I don't really use the damn things. But, you always throw people's weapons in the drink, pops? Sheesh . . . ."

"Second one in five years," I said. "First one was mine. My .45 automatic service issue."

"Go-wan, pops!" He says.

He was constantly with the 'pops' shit. I told him how I'd gone to the Rip Van Dam one night in . . . 'forty . . . 'forty-eight, yes, just before I got my first car, the Studebaker. I went right after work and was a bit, shall we say, over-served? I went on to the Elks and got into a fight with somebody. Well, George Bolster . . . you remember George? The photographer? Jesus. What am I saying? You don't remember anything, because you weren't there. I'm asking a goddamned machine if it remembers Bolster. Get the padded wagon. Anyway, Bolster got me to go home, sleep it off. He was a good man. He could say something like that to me and I respected him, because I knew he respected me. But I was young, so I went home to get my .45 instead, so I could go back and kill the guy. Fortunately, the walk home sobered me up enough. I, I came to my senses. The next day I drove to the Hudson and threw it in—holster, ammunition and all.

He was sarcastic. "Well I never woulda thrown away my service revolver."

"It's easy to kill somebody when you're trained," I said.

"Yeah, I suppose, dad. I never did." He starts to bless himself, you know, make the sign of the cross, grunts in pain and then his arm drops.

I said to him, "Junior, you've busted something." He ignores me. Younger guys onboard did, too, unless you barked at'em. Four years older than them and they called me the Old Man. I asked him if we were going to be out all night because I had mass the next day. Feast of the Assumption?

He told me not to worry! I'd be first at the rail and first at the cup. That's what he said. It's funny the things that are mileposts in your memory. I can see in my mind's eye going stretches with him smoking—my Luckies. Natch. Out of the blue he says, "So, you're doing the kneeling routine Sundays again, popsie? Funny. You never went in Saratoga. Even when your wife converted."

If I hadn't been so angry, I would have had the sense to be scared. I said something to the effect that little shits who smoke OPs and cracked wise could get their mouth cracked. Or maybe they just wanted me to drive back to Fort Edward.

He whines in that frigging accent, "Aw, geeze, Jah-gee, get a sense a you-mah, pally. I'm payin' you enough to crack wise a little witcha, ain't I? Huh? Huh?" Sticks his face over so I can get another big look at it and has this big boyish grin. Another memory milestone.

And here's another. I relaxed a little, asked how in hell he knew about Jane. He says he always keeps track of things. "Useful things." I can hear him saying it. "Useful things. Never-know-when-they-might-be-needed things." Now I had the sense to be scared. He was droning on. "Just the way my mind's built, I guess. I like facts. You came to Saratoga from Mechanicville in December of 'forty-six, started at MacFinn's, in the fall of 'forty-seven, stopped in the summer of 'fifty-two. I know why you stopped. . . ." He was pretending to try to tune the station in a little better and be nonchalant and things were just not right. Just . . . not . . . right. I had this uneasy feeling in the center of me. I should've listened to my gut. God . . . God, God, God.

Anyway, sorry, lost in thought. So, I said to him, "I wanted a store of my own." He was quiet. "Didn't want to work for Jim Leary anymore. Be connected with all that anymore."

And then he said something I almost missed because he said it in an exhale, as he was looking out of his window. But I will never, never, never forget it. He says, "None of us get that luxury." Christ. All these things screaming at me to turn around and head the wagon home. But, oh no, not George A. Not Mr. Gotta-Have-the-Money. I ignored all those things until later. I guess I was anxious to be distracted. I tried to lighten it up a little. "Hey, Junior," I said to him. "How about you? Tell me about yourself."

Not much to tell. He's from Attleboro, Massachusetts. I ask him his last name. McCarthy, he says, and makes a show of hauling out his wallet and license. Big St. Christopher's medal in the glascene window. He leaves it on his knee.

I never remember hearing anyone say his last name, in Saratoga, probably because the only time I ever spoke to him when he was in MacFinn's to buy cellophane and scotch tape. I told him a lot of people have pieces of paper that say anything they want. "You must use a half a dozen aliases," I say. He shrugs, winces. I said, "McCarthy. Irish. Hey, I'm Irish."

"So I've noted," he says, and leans forward to show me that he's thumping his forehead with his left index. I want to call him a fuckhead, but I don't. I act like I have a sweet kiss ready for him. "What County?" I ask. He says Cork. I said he didn't look Irish. He says, "I'm part Irish, Georgie. Like you." He's *really* like a filing cabinet, this boy. And I *really, really* don't like that. He had someth . . . .

Sorry. That was embarrassing. Had to puke. Jesus. Guess you heard that. Sorry. This is really, really starting to hurt.

We drove awhile. He was fiddling with the dials again. This program came on and I remember so distinctly barking, "Leave it," because the announcer was rehashing the news and mentioned possible repercussions for Senator Joseph McCarthy. I laughed into the windshield. "Hey! McCarthy? You related to Senator McCarthy, Harry?"

You will not believe what came next! I, hell, I can't even describe it. He rumbled like a volcano . . . like this . . . then he *exploded!* "That phony fuck. Red-baiting bastard, like that bastard MacArthur. *Another* phony fuck."

I told him I was in Squadron One in the Philippine Liberation landing with MacArthur when he retook the Philippines. Commanding Officer of PT 27. We came right into Manila not long after he made his return speech.

"Oh, whoopee. 'I have returned.' Gee whiz. Comes after 'I shall return.' Yeah, yeah, yeah. Big show. Blowhard. When they snuck him and his goddamn family out in those PTs, it's a pity the Japs didn't sink his fucking ship. 'I shall return'? Oh! Be still my heart." I could have been annoyed, but I was enjoying needling Junior so much I slowed the car just a little to give him a moment to ramble and said, "What'd he do? Burn your house down?"

Now, you *really* couldn't have believe . . . Oh! Oh . . . Sorry for *gasping*. I . . . I . . . can't catch . . . my breath! Unh . . . hunh. There . . . there.

Okay. Sorry again. Well, anyway, he was banging the dash with his left hand. I thought he'd break the windshield wiper button off. I told him to simmer and pulled the car over. I look at him. He was looking at his hands. He says, in this drippy voice, "Father and mother were in Washington in 'thirty-two and MacArthur burned their shanty down. All father was there for was his bonus. MacArthur tear-gassed them." He went on about the Bonus Army being hunted like criminals.

Of course, what did I know about that in 'thirty-two? I was, what? Thirteen? Mm, that's right, thirteen when this was going on? I had two good jobs, delivering papers and helping Slicky Joyce with his booze. I was a kid. I didn't really know about MacArthur. But *then* Harry says, "You know, it actually wasn't even MacArthur chasing him. It was that bastard Eisenhower."

Now that? *That* got under my skin. I told Harry he'd better go easy. Ike was a hero. But Harry never heard me. He just ranted on, "Chased them on horseback. Called 'em Reds! My father a Red? He was destroyed. I remember his face after that."

Well, he had opened the door, so I walked right in. "No. No, you don't remember squat about that, Junior." I said that really slowly. "Not at twenty-five, even at twenty-eight. Not unless you were a genius at three or six. Not unless. . . " I let it dangle. He's looking at me very intently. *Very.* Eyes not blinking, staring straight into mine. I'd see that in him. I saw it before, on deck. More times'n I'd ever wanted to.

"Not unless?" he asks.

I had a roll of nickels in my pocket and gripped it with my left fist really hard. Even my weaker left jab with that would be good. I took my hand out of my pocket. I made my voice very flat and even. "Not unless you're lying to me, Harry. Not unless you're lying."

CHAPTER 5

Well sir, Mr. Dooley, I remember him laughing and trying to brush it off. I'm telling you he was so upset he stuttered. "I–I–I m-m-meant. . ."

I laughed at him like this, made my voice really taunting, and mimicked his stutter, "Y-y-you m-m-meant what, J-J-Junior?"

Without even looking to see where the switch is, because I already know, I reach up and turn on the inside lamp so I can see what he's doing. His face was all red. I could see the veins sticking out on his neck and forehead. But he got himself under control by getting cocky, and he said, "I remembered watching his face years later. Whenever he told about it. Whadayah writin' a book? Kiss my ass'n make it a love story."

"No. No, no, no, no, no. Sorry, I tell'im. "No, things just don't add up. Just *don't* add up. Forget about his face and all that. You said you followed *The Shadow* from the start? You *couldn't've*. It began in *'thirty. I* remember it. When *I* was eleven. That would've made you *one,* maybe four." He started to say something and I told him to stow it. "I know because I was still just a paperboy, because it was the summer before I went to work for Slicky Joyce. That was nineteen thirty. In 'thirty-*one* I worked as a paperboy *and* for Slicky at his distillery."

Yeah. Goddamn right I remember it. Summer of 'thirty? All I did was deliver papers. To Slicky's speak, Betty Redtop's, and my regulars in Mickeyville. By the next summer, I'd lost most of them. On that one street by the cemetery, all but one house was foreclosed on. Nineteen-thirty was the last time I summered at Uncle Mike's farm in Eagle Bridge. And I remember that because Annie bitched because somebody else had to do my paper route and I lost the money. Meaning she lost the money, because I always gave it to her. The summer of 'thirty I listened to radio, a big deal out on the farm, radio. I was still just a boy. My last summer as just a boy.

He told me I was taking things too literally. Called me "pops" again. He was talkin' big, but he was scared now. I could smell it. "Yes, Junior, I am taking things literally. And here's a little something to stuff in your ditty bag. You were in the service. You said you wouldn't *give* up your service revolver—said it like you had one." I held up a finger and yelled, "*Don't* interrupt me. When I said that it's easy to kill somebody when you're trained how to, you didn't say, 'I was never trained how to.' You said you never did. Meaning you *were* trained. What's more, sonny, you were in the Navy," I tell him. "You call the toilet a head, my underwear skivvies and said your V-8 could haul a DE. I know what a DE is and, Bucky, you do, too."

He had his hand on the door. I knew he was reaching for something, but couldn't figure what. I clenched that roll of nickels in my left and grabbed his shirt with my right. "And you said you met me in 'forty-seven. You couldn't've been eighteen in 'forty-seven. Eighteen and already a pro? You weren't eighteen then, especially since I know in my gut you were in the War. I *know* you were in the War and I got a roll a nickels in my hand that says you were the War and you are at least 30, but I think older'n'that."

Whatever he was doing, trying to do, with his right hand, he gave it up. I remember his eyes were like saucers. He pointed at his smokes and I nodded okay and told him not to try any crap. He was lighting one up, hands shaking, and said something like, "So I'm a little older. So I like to be a little younger. I look younger. I can pass for younger. I get more tail that way."

He's calming down and I'm watching his face. He's doing a lot of thinking and I want to keep him on his toes. "What's the lighter?" I take it from him and light a Lucky. I point the lighter at his face. It's got the Seabees insignia, doesn't it? You guys and your souvenirs. And don't give me any horseshit about borrowing it."

"Actually," he said, "that was given me by a friend. But you got the rest right. You're good." I pointed to my head and said to him, "Useful things." He gave me one of those shit-eating grins, but he didn't realize that my filing cabinet had more surprises in it. But I kept those files in the drawer. I figured if I could get him to be straight with me, fine. I thought to myself as we sat and smoked that he'd probably lied a lot on a regular basis, given his line of work. Besides, anybody who torches buildings for a living isn't playing with a full deck anyway.

It was getting late and he was really getting antsy. "Come on, Georgie. I have to get to my dolly, slip her her rocks and we'll head south." I remember he said, in this real demanding tone, "And lemme have my lighter back."

"Natch," I said and threw it his way. He went to grab it and let out a grunt. I guess his arm was for real.

"*Hey!* You fuckin' moron," he bellows at me. "You know that dash has five coats of hand rubbed paint on it? You trying to mar the finish?" I got really angry. As he bent over to try to get the lighter, I grabbed him by the shirt, and when I did I saw his skin. Just below the collar line. He had a tee shirt on, Navy regulation, not one of these dago tee shirts. Oh, God. It was so scarred. I took my eyes off it immediately—immediately!—so he wouldn't see that I'd seen. I hadn't seen burns like that since I was in the VA hospital to have my legs done after the war. So many guys with burns like that.

He sat bolt upright and looked at me hard. His voice was older than the ages and it had this—how do I put this?—this calm rage in it. "Don't you ever put your hands on me again, Mister—unless you plan to kill me." I told him to relax and said nobody barked orders at me. Truth was, he was a little frightening. Something in his tone and the way he held himself. I mean, I knew he wasn't all there, setting stuff on fire for a living, but there was something in the way his eyes looked so empty. I'd seen it in men who'd been out there too long. My cousin Joe said I looked like that the last time I saw him in the Pacific. And then he was dead.

Well, anyways. I slapped the Studebaker in gear and we pulled off. My God, what a car! It had power like the boats I had. Three Packard diesels, all lined up and synchronously geared. What a wake it threw!

We drove about a mile in quiet. I was itching to know more. I said something . . . . What the hell was it? Oh, of course. "Hey, Junior," I said to him, "as long as we're getting ready to have a giant weenie roast, let's tell some campfire stories, huh—like why we're burning a building that hasn't had a customer in a year? Hasn't had any gambling since, what? 'Fifty-one?'"

He was still quiet for another minute and then he laughs and says, "You're something else, George." He sounded older. And, then, just as if he were speaking about, oh, getting coffee stains on your tie, he says there's no sense telling me, because it would just get us both killed. Those were his words. "It would just get us both killed." Then he says, he said, really slowly, "You can never tell anybody you came with me, George," pauses, then says in a voice about as dry as the dust bowl, "You haven't, have you?"

Phewwwww . . . . A question like that really shakes you. I mean . . . really. Really. I tried sound sarcastic to cover my jumpiness and said, "Yeah. I called the editors at *The Saratogian*, the *Daily News*. I'm on my two-way wrist radio working to get Ed Murrow." Then I said, "Of course I didn't. Who would I call? *Who*? *Why*?"

He says, "Who's on first. Why's on second."

"Honestly. Who would I call? Frank Costello? Huh? Lansky?" He didn't say anything. If only I had really listened to his voice, his tone. I would have never, ever have gone down to Saratoga. Ever.

I was *really* uncomfortable now. I tried to lighten it up again. I said something like, "Your name really is Harry McCarthy?" He laughed this big laugh. It's still something to remember. And then his voice was boyish again. He said, "Goddamnit, man! I'm tellin' yoo, Jah-gee, you're sump'in' else. Whatta setta balls!" He said it would probably be best if I didn't know *that* either. I was, shall we say, a tad too sensitive at this point to ask if *that* would also get us killed. H'yock, h'yock.

He let out this big sigh and lit another Lucky. Christ. Glad I'd grabbed a carton from the store. "All, right," he said in this really annoyed voice. He tells me it was the name he used for here and for his sales. And he purposely hadn't sold too much around here, he confided. It was just a good cover. Better for the city where it was easier to hide among more people. I didn't understand what he meant and I asked him, "Saratoga Springs?" That city? And here I nearly decked him. He called me a hick jerk and said, no, he means Manhattan. "Drop dead, Harry. I've seen more of the world than you."

He muttered something I took for an apology'n said that in Saratoga he sells only to those who know and who are a good cover. "You'd be surprised how many don't know who I am. The ones who know are the ones who *need* to know." Wasn't that a funny way of putting it? I did not listen, even though I heard. I remember he said something like, "You just don't want to show up so much that people begin liking you and asking you home for dinner or asking you all about your home life and all that."

I couldn't resist and I said, "So, tell me more about your home life, Mr. Kilroy."

I heard a laugh come out of the dark and a "Wise ass." I heard the lighter snap shut, as we pulled south onto Route 9. He pretty much repeated what he'd said before, little extra here and there. He added he only had one sister. A surprise. Two wasn't very big for a Catholic family. "Mother, Mom, had complications after my sister. Couldn't have any more. But, hey-hey, you're an only child, right, Georgie?" I told him my father died at five and he suddenly recites, as if from a book, "And your mother remarried. And before you ask, nobody told me." One time I guess I'd said her last name's Fitzpatrick. He put it together. Two and two make four.

I said she was 34 and had me by C-section. I repeated what she always says—said—whenever she tells this, 'And I went down the Valley of Death for George.'

He laughed. "Yea though I walk through the Valley of the Shadow of Death . . . . Yeah, and she probably didn't find any comfort in your old man's rod and staff after that." He laughed at that. I didn't.

There was something I asked him. Let me think for a minute what the hell it was. It was important. Oh! I asked . . .   What the hell's that? [*A telephone is ringing in the background.*]

Oh, Christ. The frigging phone. "Hello? Mmm-hmm. Oh, that's too bad. Mmm-hmm. Tonight? Now? *Right* now? God. What? No, no. It's okay. No, it's all right. No, I'm sure. Sure I'm sure. I'll meet you there."

Oh, sure. I wanted to go to the store right now. It was my dream. I really want to get back into my pants and hop in the car. Yes, indeedy I do.

"Do I? Honey! `Deed I do."

I oughta have my. . . have my head examined. I tell her not to get so low on that script that she runs out—and every goddamn *frigging* time she runs out at some oddball hour and I end up . . . .

[*Sounds of sighing and profanity. Tape recorder is shut off.*]

CHAPTER 6

[*Tape recorder on again. There are long pauses, some mumbling and words slightly slurred.*]

Woof. Knew I shouldn't've gone. Tch, tch, tch. Nearly died. Yes, sirree, Bob. Close one. Woof. Close. Doan know how I missed those Mounties. Goddamn fender all bashed in. Let's get a brew. "Peg o' my heart, I . . . ."

Where was I? Oh, my God, my arm hurts. This is not good. I was where? Lessee. I said to him you were in the US Navy . . . . No wait a minute. I said that already. Jesus. I can't remember what I was *talking about*! Oh, God, I don't think I dare rewind this. No. *Shit.* Let me see . . . if I can recon . . . struct this. I said about his being in the Navy. I remember I said, I mean, I asked him about his real name. Oh, oh, oh. Wait, wait, *wait*! I remember what I *didn't* tell. I *didn't* tell that when I had grabbed him by the shirt, I saw his skin. That's right. I said , uh, saw . . . . Slow down, boy. Said that . . . I . . . saw his skin below the collar line. *Unbelievable* scarring. Brother. Only time I saw burn scars like that . . . in Pearl City. Oh, yeah. The VA hospital later. To have my legs done. A lotta reconstruction. Lotta shrapnel. When we loss—lost—the boat. Still have a lot of shrapnel. Look at my legs. *Lookat'em*! Stuff still coming out after forty-three years. Right here? I got hit here with . . . errp! Sorry. Get any on you? Hah, hah, hah. Got hit here with a hawser when I worked on the dredges at eighteen. Poor bassard. . . Poor bastard in front of me was cut in two. Saved my life. I was outta work a long time.

All right. All hands! Let's get back at it. Yeah, sure. Can't even talk. Let's . . . get . . . back . . . at . . . it. God, wha-wazz-I saying? Should take notes er-sump-in. . . . [*A long period with no sound follows.*]

What? All right? Must have fallen asleep. All right? Let's see. We got off, um, 197 by Howard Johnson's. I wanted a drink but he says "Later!" Punk. Mmmmmm. . . What then? C'mon. What? Okay. I say he talked about his family? Oh, right. Right, right, right. We're heading down Route 9 and it's the old three-lane concrete road, okay? And the car's going, kah-*thump*, kah-*thump*, kah-*thump* on the concrete, and by the time we're passing down by Aust's Drive-In he's talking about his, um, about his service. "South Pacific," he says. Me . . . errp! Sorry to belch again.

Me too, I say. South Pacific, I mean. "I know," he says. "People I knew in town, they knew about your service record. It was, um, quite a record, pops."

Sure was. Damn that hurts. I toll'im he could drop the stops puff. Goddamn. Drop the, the. . . Shit, I can't even pronounce anything. The pops stuff. Drop the pops stuff. I told him I couldn't be that much older than he was. "Habit," he said. We're driving with the windows down now. Son of a bitch actually had, uh, air conditioning in it. 'Magine that. Woof. I'm roasting. Lemme splash some water in my face.

Okay. Back again. Let me see. We're almost to the Brown Log Inn now. I ask him some more about where he served. What he served on. "On the Dennis J. Buckley," he says.

"Oh, was that a DE?" I tried to ask that real innocently, but he answers me that it was a DD/DDR. They sailed it out of Virginia and into the Pacific, but he transferred off at Midway. "Did I pass the test?" he asks me.

I ignored him and asked if he had a rosary. I needed to say a few decades before we got to the Piping Rock. He didn't answer and I said it would only take me a minute, minute and half to say'em, and I'd be done. He snapped open the glove compartment, reached in, handed me one and barked, "Don't lose it!" I should've just said that rosary right then and there and turned around, just turned around when we pulled into the lot of the Brown Log Inn. Just drove away. Oh God, oh God, why didn't I turn around? Why didn't I? Why? Why? Why?

[There were *gasping noises and choking sounds. The tape stopped and apparently the time elapsed is one night. He has restarted the tape the next morning, which is a Sunday. It is likely either the weekend of the 11th or the 18th as he does not mention the Fourth of July.*]

Okay. Let's see what we can do in a day. Where'd I leave off? Where's my pad? Thank God for all these Pfizer notepads the salesmen all leave. Jennie always gets, got, millions of them working in the doctor's office. God, she loved these Sundays. We'd go to church and then down to the pharmacy. Have coffee. She'd get her *New York Times*. I can see her stretched out on the sun porch with it. I will never understand how is it that she retired in December and was diagnosed with the Big C in January. Father Bass said it was test of our faith. She told me he could go fuck himself. She had never said that word in all the time we were together. God, she hated him so.

Where was I? God, my handwriting's awful. It was so bad, the physicians—damn, that coffee's hot! They said that with handwriting that bad I should have been a physician. I would've been a damn good one. I remember when Chick Holloway came in complaining about heartburn. I looked at him in the prescription room and called the ambulance. Doctor Tom said I saved his life. My best diagnosis will be on myself and who will even know it?

I don't understand this note. "Five or ten minutes." What is that? "Five or ten minutes" what? What did I mean . . . ? Mm-hm, I was at the Brown Log—that's it. We were about five or ten minutes out from the Brown Log Inn, and nothing was adding up. Okay? *Nothing*—nothing, nothing, *nothing*—was adding up. The guy was like a bad onion. Peel back a layer and there's another layer. And each stinks more than the last. I don't know why I had this compulsion to find out, but I had to. I had to *peel* the onion, peel away each and every layer. Who's involved with this? I mean, who am I involved with? Who's hired him that he's so scared? Well, okay, I wasn't *totally* stupid. I mean, I knew the mob owned every casino down there and I knew Costello, Adonis and Lansky owned Piping Rock. Or *did* own, I should say. They'd just sold it. And there you go. That's making me wonder why. The club's *dead.* It's been *sold.* Been closed since—what? 'Fifty-one? No, 'fifty.

Why is Harry . . . ? Okay, why are *we* getting ready to burn down the Piping Rock? I can't even say those words without the chills running up and down my spine. But, back then? I was thinking something different. I knew he was getting paid, but what's the point if there's *nothing* left? No connection. It was like all those casinos—Piping Rock, Riley's, Newman's—just washed up after Kefauver. Before that they were everything. From the time I was a busboy at the Colonial in '36 and Jennie worked at Brown's, those places were night life and high society to us. Why, they were like being in Manhattan to us. What did we know? After the war, when we'd moved to Saratoga, the first thing we did after we got our first car was drive out and take color snapshots of them. We even got to go to them during the season, even though we were locals. Oh, heavens! They couldn't let the local riffraff in. Well, we got in! Saw all the acts. And, then, poof! They're gone.

So, you see my question? Why? So, well, what happened next is, well, I just can't explain what happened next. Hang on. Let me get a coffee. Oh, hell, that's right. Let me walk and talk.

[*Garbled noise. Some dialogue lost.*]. . . traffic seemed to be getting heavier. I remember glancing over and shifting the rearview so I was looking at his face as a series of lights lit it up. He was older than he was saying. I didn't expect I'd say it, but it just flowed out: "Harry? What's all this about? You're not from Attleboro. You're from Brooklyn, or somewhere in that general vicinity. Your accent's all wrong."

"Whaddayah know about accents? Huh? Huh? Whaddayah know about anything?"

"I stayed in Brooklyn at the St. George in 'forty-six when I worked for E.R. Squibb."

He was really saracastic. "Aww, the boy's a linguist! Let's all mawch around the breakfast table, Aunt Fannie! He went to Haw-vad."

I told him if he were from Attleboro he would've said "Let's all *match* around the breakfast table, *Ont* Fannie!" And Harvard should've been pronounced "Hah-vahd." I came to Mickeyville when I was five speaking with a Boston accent and even at that age I got *shit* for it.

He tried some crap about not originally being from Attleboro, but I told him to fuck off and said he sounded New York, like the Dead End Kids. Kah-*boom*! He explodes again. What *was* this, he wants to know? Crime Busters? And starts saying, "Huh? HUH?" and slamming on the dash each time. His temper was really on my nerves. I was jumped up and losing my will! And he keeps saying, "Huh? Huh?" About the fifth "Huh?" I really laid into that bastard. "*I* wanna know what it's *all* about. I want to know *why*.'

"These are the questions of life, Georgie."

He was so condescending. I blew! "Shut up with that crap! And shut that *shit* off on the radio or get something else on there a man can listen to that makes sense." He punched a button and something softer came on. I was still hollering, "*I want to know who I'm working for!* This is crazy! *Insane!* I'm getting ready to burn down a building and I don't know anything about why, I don't about *who* and I sure as hell know less and less about *you* as the night goes by!"

"Take it easy, pally," he says in that I'm-gonna-calm-you-down voice.

"Don't *pally* me!"

Oh, man that hurts. Oh, unh, unh. Breathe, George. Uhn . . . breathe! Breathe, please. Sorry. Wow. Sorry. This is killing me. Unh . . . anyway, I'm screaming, "You say you're twenty-five and then you're not. You say you remember things you couldn't unless you were my age, *maybe* more. You remember radio shows you couldn't *possibly* remember and, and you have memories of your parents that have to be first hand . . . you say you're from Massachusetts and then you say you're not." And he started to say something and I put up my hand, like this, right at his face, and said, "No! *Don't* say you've explained it all! *Don't!* You haven't. First you weren't in the War, then you were in the War, but it doesn't sound like much duty, but then I see a burn scar like I haven't seen since sick bay in Pearl City. . ."

Woof! I'm shouting! Hah, hah, hah! I'm shouting now like I did then! Oh, God, I'm as upset as I was then! And I was so upset back then I almost missed that his voice became really flat, but the tone of it just suddenly jerked me back into reality. He said, all soft and level, "What are you talking about?" Really controlled. I knew he was like a bomb ready to go. Any second. "What are you talking about, George?"

"Your scar. It's a burn. Burns like I saw on the guys we'd pick up out of the sea from exploding ships. Fuel oil burns. Maybe flamethrower burns. I saw them in Pearl City. In sickbay. I saw them in the VA hospital afterwards."

"Sooooo?" with a low tone, through clenched teeth.

"So, a burn like that is a big deal. But *nothing* with you is a big deal. *Nothing* is ever really complete. Maybe you didn't get it in service. Maybe you got it in prison, instead of serving your country like a man . . ."

And, boys and girls, *that* did it! Oh, baby! *He blew!* He moved toward the glove compartment. What the hell's he got in there, I'm wondering? A sap? He wouldn't sap me while I'm driving? Well, maybe. I don't think Emily Post ruled on when you sap a guy. Remember, ladies, never sap the driver of a moving vehicle. Well, I couldn't take that chance. There was no one around us. I was doing over sixty and I jerked the steering wheel hard to the right and the car went up on two wheels. Woof! He started falling my way! I was counting on those weights and hoping they were really there. Then I jerked it again to the left and the car slams down and I heard him bang up against the passenger door with a grunt and start swearing. I pointed straight into a field, hoping to Christ that there wasn't a drainage ditch.

God, I can see it! We shoot into that field. I brace my left hand and jam the clutch in and hit the brakes and all the while I can hear him hollering and swearing and grunting while he's bouncing all over the car, because we hit these corn rows! It's a goddamned plowed field! And we're bumping and jerking across and suddenly I jam to a stop, let the clutch up while it's in gear and the engine stalls dead!

He's still trying to dig into that frigging glove compartment and I don't have a thing to stop him. So I brace my back against my door, hold the steering wheel with my left hand and the back of the seat with my right and twist myself around in the seat and shoot my right leg in a kick at him. He's quick. He takes some of it, but he dodges a lot, the fucker. He's too quick! Now he's got the door open and I'm right after him, right over his seat, 'cause I figure I'd better get the bastard before he gets *me!* A wonder I didn't nut myself on the shift. The lights come on in the car and as I'm passing the glove compartment all I see's paper. No sap. No nothing. I don't know *what* to do. But I stay after him and as I come out, he wheels on me and charges!

Thank *God!* You can always take advantage of somebody charging at you. I fought too many street fights not to know. He's coming at me and I step aside like a toreador so I'm on his right side, his weak side, and I even let him get a sideways shot at me into my stomach with his left arm. *Kee-rist,* it hurts! My *God,* he's strong! But I know now that I have him. I seize that arm, and bend it in back of him. I grab his hair and just use that momentum and shove the bastard's face first onto the front seat and scramble up to put my knees on his back. Up near his neck, so that I can smother him to death if I have to. And it looks like I might have to. I keep the pressure up so that he knows he's smothering. I hear the muffled screaming. I go just a *little* bit more and then jerk his head up.

"Don't kill me! Don't kill me!" he's screaming at me. "I'm okay. I'm *okay!*" He just lost his head, he says. Yeah. I nearly lost mine. Thought I was going to kill him. That was frightening. He kept promising he was okay. "I'm *okay!*"

I don't why—probably because I'd been in the same position and made the same promise—but I let him up. I helped him get around sitting up in the seat. I'm glad he's being the calm boy, because I'm winded and I'm, I'm shaky and I didn't know how much longer I could've kept up against him. Meanwhile, now that it's quieter, I realize the radio's still going and the blasted *windshield* wipers are on, too. You know? The radio didn't turn off with the engine in those days. Neither did the wipers. We must've hit the button on the dash. And the radio's blaring *Heart of My Heart.* He reached over and snapped it off, saying, "Goddamn that fucking song," and he shut off the wipers and slammed the glove compartment shut.

I reminded him that I threw the gun in the canal. I was trying not to let myself gasp too much.   "I'm not a killer," he said in a quiet way. "I'd've just used it to scare you off. You're a strong boy." He let out this big sigh. "Jesus, Mary and Joseph. I'm not a killer."

"Yeah, and you're not a Catholic, either," I said. I was still standing close to him. I braced myself.

"What?" he asked me. Didn't look at me. His jaw muscle twitched, but that's all.

"You heard me. You're not a Catholic. You're not bad at it, but it's the little things. Such as, it takes a *long* time to do a decade of the rosary. Long. And, Catholics don't take wine at the altar. "First at the cup"? Unh-unh. Oh, yeah, and tomorrow's not the Feast of the Assumption. It was yesterday, Junior."

Phewwww . . . I swear to you, at that moment, I thought he'd gone nuts, because he didn't get angry, didn't, ah, um, *erupt* like I thought he would. No. Just sat there for a lonnnnng minute and then started to laugh. And he laughed and laughed and laughed and it built up and in ten seconds he was laughing like a *loon*. I swear to you, I thought he'd just come out of Poughkeepsie. It was scary!

And then he just stopped. *Bam!* Which was, shall we say, just a little disconcerting? And, um, and his eyelids were almost closed, kind of fluttering shut, if that makes any sense, and his head started nodding slightly up and down. And then he said in this voice that is someone else's—it just raised the hairs on the back of my neck, I want to tell you— just not his voice, "No, not a Catholic. You're right. I'm not a Catholic. And I'm not Junior, George. I'm forty-five years old. I'm definitely *not* your junior." And he just kept staring out over the field with his head nodding slightly and his eyelids still moving in that same way.

CHAPTER 7

I remember wondering to myself if I'd hit him in a way somehow that made him strange, because either I'd lost my mind—okay?—or he'd lost his. I just didn't know what to say to all that. I mean, what do you say to that? Just, just. . . well, you know. And finally I said that I'd better turn the engine over so the battery wouldn't run down.

I went around to the driver's side of the car and as I was opening the door, I heard him say, in this calm and *very* different voice that I didn't have to worry about it, because he had extra batteries installed in the trunk. I remember him saying, "I could light Ebbets Field with the power I have in here." I said okay, and he was quiet, and then he said, "But it might be best if you were to get in and close the doors. So that we don't attract attention." Again, this, this strange voice, like this, ". . .might be best if you were." It was like somebody else was in the car. I've got goose bumps thinking of it even now. Even now. By the Jesus. Oh. Let me have a drink here. Mmm, that's good.

I reached acrosst him and closed the door on his side and then on mine. Then started up the car, but left the lights off. I mean, I didn't want to offend the guy, but that stuff about lighting up Ebbets Field I didn't buy a bit. Of course, later, I'd find out what a mistrusting bunghole I really was, but I, ah, I didn't feel, shall we say, in a trusting state at that point. I never should have been at any point. Except about the batteries.

I found my pack of Luckies on the floor. They were a bit bent, but not bowed. I can still smell that fresh tobacco smell. Mmmm. I offered him one and we sat smoking. I stood it for as long as I could, then I said, "Look. I don't understand."

"It's as I said." I remember him saying that, just that way, in that strange voice, "It's as I said." And then he let out this gigantic exhale and said, "It's self-explanatory. I'm forty-five years old. I'm not a Catholic. And I'm not from Attleboro, although my maternal grandparents were from that area. And I do remember *The Shadow*, first hand, George, and do recall Father and Mother being tear-gassed out of their Hooverville. Quite vividly. I was a man then."

I think I said he didn't have . . . wait a minute, yes I did, I did say . . . . No, I didn't. Doesn't matter. He didn't have that nasal Brooklyn accent anymore. I, I know you're gonna laugh when I say this, but he sounded like . . . well, wait. Wait a minute, wait a minute, wait a minute. My thoughts are getting ahead of me. I didn't mean I noticed he didn't have that Brooklyn kind of accent anymore. He still had a New York sounding accent, but—and *this* is where you're going to laugh, okay?—but it sounded like FDR's.

He said, "I just couldn't keep it up any longer with you, Georgie. Sorry. Habit. George. You're just too bright, too perceptive." Not blowin' my horn here, folks. It's what he said. He rolled the window down and flicked the butt out into the night and let out this gigantic sigh. He can dance around people, he says, but I'm too much like him. Collecting *useful* information. Couldn't deny it, I told him. And then he laughed. Sounded like FDR, I tell you.

I understood him. It took work, planning a big job and having a lot on his mind. And then I'm pounding him with questions that he's got to dodge or come up with answers. Then I nearly kill him in the car—his words, okay?—and he's rattled. And bang! I hit him with this Catholic thing and, as he said, "Buddy, that was all she wrote. You're really annoying, buddy." Yeah, that's what he said. "You're really annoying, buddy."

I waited a minute more while he complained and then I asked very softly, "Who are you?" I think I was afraid to find out. Not sure I even would find out once I heard the answer.

"I'm Harry Fennington. I really am a Harry—thank God, because it makes it easier when I'm using that other ID—but it's a bit more formal that just Harry Fennington."

And, and he laughed a jerky laugh that I'd never heard him laugh in all the time that I'd known him. It was like someone else'd come in the car and taken his place. Guess I said that?

Anyways, he says, "No, it's Harrison Valentine Pierce Fennington," and then he let out that weird laugh again—I was getting the heebie-jeebies 'cause it, well, it wasn't him. Sorry to dwell on this. And then he says, "The second." And then he added, and I'll always remember this, he added "And, *please*, don't laugh at my name. Although sometimes I do when I say it aloud like that. Harrison Valentine Pierce Fennington the second. It's like I'm two people." I have to say I think he was telling the truth. *Nobody* could make up a, well, you know, a *fruity* name like that. And it really seemed like I had two people in the car.

If I said anything else, I don't remember. All I do remember was at some point saying, "How can you be forty-five? You can't be forty-five." Christ, I remember sounding like some friggin' ten-year-old. "How can you be forty-five? You can't be forty-five." It's a wonder I didn't add, "gee willickers!"

We puffed on the smokes a while. I didn't push him. Then he said—and oh, God, I just cannot forget the way he spoke—"Well, there are two things at work, here, George. One is that I was most fortunate to have inherited a very young face from my two parents . . . who were both extremely youthful looking all their lives." Listening to him was like listening to Adolph Monjou on the radio. "You above all should know—Mendel and his peas and all that. And the second thing is that I had a great plastic surgeon. These burns—here let me flip on the light. . ." He pulled up his shirt at this point and I nearly puked. God, Jane hates that word. I almost did. They covered part of his arms and chest and back. He said he was lucky. He said, "You were right the first time. It was an oil burn, but I'd taken a hit in the Adriatic. Didn't keep me out of the Liberation of Paris, though." He said it was more superficial than it looked.

And I just stared. I tried not to gawk and asked him, "You weren't in the Pacific?" I was glad he couldn't see me. He'd really hit me a wallop and I was nursing my chest. Yes, he was, he said. The first burn wasn't bad but he made it worse the second time—in the Pacific. You'll understand—I mean, I'll get to that in a minute. Hang on. Anyways, he was in great demand in both theaters. He had "*special talents.*" And I said, "You mean, torching things?"

He said, "Exactly." That was in February of 'forty-two. My last semester at Union. He said he wasn't as careful then, as he is now. I mean, "now" as in nineteen fifty-four. I'm in `fifty-four now. You know what I mean. He got caught out on Long Island. Somebody ratted on him about a warehouse job. He was being held for transfer in Oyster Bay and the local constable recognized him. Put in a good word'n'Harry was given the "choice" of going in the service. They dropped all the charges and in he went.

I asked him what he was doing in Oyster Bay. It didn't mean a lot to me. I mean, I knew Teddy Roosevelt was from there. But he assumed it meant something to me and he said, "Yeah. My family goes back to the sixteen hundreds in that area. Dutch and English. Old family. Old money."

What the hell? One minute he's a wiseass kid. The next he's older than I am, serious and mature and, oh, hell, I don't know. Just not making any sense. I told him flat out. "I'm starting to smell a particular substance that's remarkably like horseshit. Big steaming piles of it."

He gets all self-righteous and says "No-no-no-no-no-no-no." Not so. I wanted the truth and he was going to give me the truth. And with that he started to talk about himself. I will tell you what I remember. It's, ah, well, it's really quite amazing. I recall the tone of his voice. It was actually a bit deeper. Maybe not. It was mellower. That's it. I couldn't get over the difference between them. Him I mean. A kid jumping around in my store and now this guy. We had this kid at Pearl City who'd been under fire— Mormon, about eighteen—his boat had taken a direct hit. He'd woke up in sick bay—the organization of which, incidentally, got *yours truly*, George A. King, a commendation for service above and beyond. Anyway, this kid'd suddenly gone from being like an eighteen-year-old to sounding and acting like his grandfather, who raised him. It lasted about a week, but it spooked us. Had that grandfatherly way and his *voice* was old. "Can I have a cup of coffee, son?" That sort of thing?

Kind of the same with Harry, but I really wasn't buying forty-five, if you know what I mean. Things were just so crazy. It'd only been a few hours and here I was, riding with Harry the Torch to Saratoga to get my first merit badge in rubbing two gas cans together. Oh, baby.

So, I ask him was Harry McCarthy anybody real? Yep. Some kid he'd been in service with. Died in 'forty-five. Talked *constantly* about himself and his family and Attleboro. He says, "It worked okay until I met you, you rotten bastard." He laughed. I was afraid to shut him up, now that he was rolling, but I was thinking about those thousand iron men. I asked him what time we had to meet his girlfriend at the Brown Log Inn and he says we better drag our freight. Wouldn't want to miss his little sweetheart and that sweet alibi she was going to give us. That made me shudder inside. "Give *us*."

He fiddled with the radio and when it warmed up, the bebop came blasting out. He grunted and fell back into the seat. I was shocked when he said, "My arm." I wondered how mucha the work I'd have t'do. He said I was pretty strong—his arms and back were killing him. I admitted he was in pretty good shape, too, but didn't let on how much he hurt *me*.

He said he was trying to tune in this station out of Baltimore and told me to punch the button nearest me. Swing suddenly came on the radio.

"What the hell's *this*," I ask him. Something called The Harley Show. 'Twenties and 'thirties music.

"Don't you like bebop?" Actually, he says, he understands it. A lot he said. It . . . how'd he put it? It's what he needed to . . . what he needed to. . . To what? "To complete the other me." That's it. That's *it!* "To complete the other me." I asked him if that was like the other kid, the real Harry McCarthy. No, he said, he made it up. This whole thing about be-bop'n'all. Made it up. But he didn't want to talk about it. Probably boring for him. Who knows? He kept snapping his fingers and saying, "This is jazz. This is *jazz! Listen!*"

He talked on about being in Chicago and going to every little club. "I knew Bennie Moten," he said. He raved on about swing and I said, "You were at Goodman's Carnegie Hall concert in 'thirty-eight."

"Little slip-up on that one?"

"A nine year-old kid from Attleboro in New York City?" I say. If he was nine, even twelve in 'thirty-eight, Mae West was still a virgin. Got a chuckle out of him with that.

What did he say to me, um . . . ? *Damn,* I can't believe I'm *forgetting* some of this! Jesus, it's *unfair.* I spent so long remembering it. I've been haunted by it. It's like after you're under fire. You want to stop being haunted by those memories, but they keep *at* you. Now you *need* that memory and it's slipping away. Um, let's see. Mmmmm. . .oh! Okay. We're riding . . . c'mon, George, get back behind the wheel. Um. *OH!* He pays me a compliment. I was *good!* 'Thirty-eight was, ah, um. . . . . an excellent year. An excellent year? No. . . . No, no, no, no! An *exquisite* year! That's it! An *exquisite* year.

"Mr. Memory! What are the Thirty-nine Steps?" No, honestly, he said it was an *exquisite* year. What a word, huh? It was an *exquisite* year, because he saw Goodman live at Carnegie Hall *and* because he burned down his family home. Yessiree, Bob. That's how he said it, over'n'over again. "I saw Goodman live at Carnegie Hall and I *burned* down the old family home." Mm-hm. "Saw Goodman live at Carnegie Hall and I burned down the old family home."

Aw, God, I should've known right then.

CHAPTER 8

I was glad I was going slow while pulling out of that field, because, I want to tell you, I think I would have driven into a *telephone* pole after hearing that. . . . Unh, hm, Unh! Sorry. Please Lord, just keep me alive till I get through this. Hail Mary . . .

I got acrosst the field—and, and that car was flowing over ruts and bumps—so, I got acrosst the field and we got up on 9 and took off in fine style. I had just popped that baby into top gear and I just couldn't—Unh!—just couldn't hold it in anymore, you know? I said, "How's seeing Benny Goodman live the same as using the old family manse for a weenie roast?" I mean, Jennie and I danced to Goodman at the Troy Armory in, what? Thirty-nine? Oh, *God*. They had huge springs under the floor and the place just *bounced*! I think I kinda stepped out on a limb here, because I remember saying, "Hey. That's kind of nuts."

Now he's upset. What'd I mean by that? What'd I mean by that? You know? Over and over. I hate when people repeat themselves. I told him that I know making a hot time in the old town tonight is his job, but doing it to the family house? Come on. You know? I didn't believe him and I told him so. Just didn't believe him.

I didn't understand, he tells me. "Got *that* right!" I told'im.

"It was sweet revenge, George. Sweet revenge." He says it over'n'over. He repeated himself a lot, especially when he got hot on a topic. No pun intended. Annoying when guys repeat what they say. He did it a lot. Anyways, it wasn't the family's house anymore, he says. It had been stolen from'em and he wasn't going to let that bastard keep it.

"Who?" I want to know.

All he said was: "My godfather." I can't even begin to tell you the hatred I heard. I am telling you, it raised goose bumps from my head to my toenails.

"Yeah, George, I hated that man for what he did to us." We were shooting down 9 at a good clip and I remember he warns me about my speed. Afraid we're going to get a ticket. Hah! He didn't seem like a nervous Nellie or anything. Still, I saw his point. I was really nervous, to be really honest. We're whizzing down the road and all I could think of is how the hell we were going to get away with this. How do we burn down a famous landmark just down the road from Saratoga Race Course *during* the racing season? I hope you won't think I'm some kind of baby'er something, but I was close to soiling my knickers. I had that loosie-goosie feeling you'd get as you'd approach an enemy ship. But I had to admit it—it was *exciting!*

Well, now that he had told me how old he was, he had to tell me who he was, and got into a big confessional mood. I'm used to this. The Father Confessor bit. Christ, I carry more secrets about my customers than Carter has pills. He said he was born in 1909, which makes him ten years older'n I am. [*The tape is damaged here. Some information is simply gone. Then the tape comes back enough to It seems that guess that George is saying that Harry's family was rich, but Harry said they weren't rich. Then the sound quality returns.*] His father was worth around five million, he says, but they're not rich. Well off. According to the rest of his family, just "*well off.*"

I was really sarcastic. "Nah," I said, "Five mil. No, that's not rich. Hell, if you were rich, you'd have lived in a boarding house on Third Street in Mechanicville." Jerk. Well off little rich boy.

I think he kind of squirmed a little on that. I mean, what I said about Mechanicville. I didn't call him a little rich boy to his face. He says that, yeah, sure, he sees my point and then he says, "You see, in *our* family, we weren't rich. Now, Father's cousin Edding, now, *he* was rich. He just had hundreds and hundreds and hundreds of millions in the 'twenties."

Was it Edding? Edward? No, Edding. That's right. Edding. Right the first time. Harry said Edding got down to his last forty million in . . . Can you imagine that? Can you? Forty mil? That's a lot of berries, boys and girls! A *lot* of berries. Anyways, when did Harry say it was? Wait, wait, wait. He said it was in, in . . . 'thirty-one—yes 'thirty-one—because I distinctly remember hearing him saying that it was when he was in Chicago. In 'thirty-one. Yeah, he was banging the dash with his left hand, which startled me. "That was it, George," he says. "They kicked the poor bastard out of his club in Ann Arbor because he just didn't have enough money. Edding drove his car off a bluff into Lake Michigan and killed himself. Shame. Poor bastard."

I told him I was near tears and might have to pull the car over to regain my self-control. Yes, it was truly a real pity. Gee willikers. If I'd known it then, I would've gone right out and taken up a collection for poor Edding's widow, bought her a chicken salad sandwich or something. H'yock, h'yo. . . Oh, God. God. Gotta get my . . . my breath.

Well, he was on a roll and ignored me. But I mean, "*poor bastard*"? Jesus Christ. Goddamn rich kids. Assuming that Harry *was* what he said he *was* —

that he *was* really a rich kid. I was convinced, but, you know, I wasn't convinced—then, anyways. So, he was on a roll and just kept right on talking. There's something in me that gets people to talk to me. Probably because they know I'll never tell. And here I am telling all.

"No," he says, "my family was old North Shore money." I told him I didn't know what that meant. Long Island, he says. North Shore Long Island, the Gold Coast. "Actually my Dad was on the Social Register. We're Episcopalians, although I understand that was kind of. . ." What was it Harry said? What *was* that word?

Holy Mary, Mother of God that hurts! Concentrate, George. He understood it was kind of, uh, phony? No. God. C'mon. Oh, yeah. Kind of an affectation. He said it was an *affectation* on his grandfather's part and was a little too *papist* for some of the family. He's prattling on to *me* like *I'm* a goddamn *Protestant* and understand it all. Anyway, he asks *me* if I don't think that being Episcopalian is kind of close to being Roman Catholic.

Wait. I don't mean "goddamn Protestant," all right? Jennie's family's all Protestant. Forget I said that. But, I mean, how the hell would . . . .?

Oh! Uh, uh, oh, Lord. I've got to. . .to stop. . .for a minute. Oh! My chest is kill . . . .

[*The recording stops and resumes later. This is very hard to transcribe. From references made it's the same day. He has had a bit to drink now.*]

Okay. Okay. All righty then. What was this guy telling me now? Let's see if I can find my pad. Let's see. What's this say? God, my handwriting's awful. Awful! All the doctors in town said I should have been a doctor, because my handwriting was so awful. I would've been a good one. I should've stayed in the service. I could become one there. Biggest mistake of my life. No, the second biggest after this.

Episcopalian. That's the word. What's this? Um, *godfather.* Oh, okay. Yup. Okay. Got it. Here it is. He said he went St. Paul's and then right off to Harvard. And as God is my witness, as the s.o.b. is telling me he's been to Harvard he bums a Lucky off me, and then in the next breath says, "Just what you'd expect, right?"

"That you'd bum a Lucky?"

Which Dr. Einstein didn't get. No, he says, he meant, that he went to Harvard from St. Paul's. Wasn't that just what you'd expect? Oh, certainly, I said. I'd planned on it for myself. But, my paper route didn't quite pan out and, besides, I had had this great offer right out of high school to follow in my late father's footsteps and go to the exclusive Great Lakes Dredge and Dock Company. I was supposed to major in coal shoveling, but had an accident and was forced to put myself through college.

He kept ignoring me. I remember asking him what the hell I would know about St. Paul's and Harvard and something like he didn't know what it was like on *my* side of the fence. I told him that. Yeah. I told him! If it hadn't've been for that paper route'n' working for Slicky Joyce, we'd've been broke. I earned more than my stepfather did as a fireman on the B&M! Poor bastard. He'd go out on a run to Boston and deadhead straight back to Mickeyville. Sixteen straight hours. *Sixteen* goddamn back breaking hours as a fireman and he'd bring home with *less* than I did. *Less! Jesus, Mary and Joseph!* And did that cause a bit of *tension*, shall we say, in the old homestead?

I told Little Lord Fauntleroy I was sorry when Prohibition ended. I was making such good money working for the Joyces.

"You really worked for Slicky as a little kid?" he asks me. I shouldn't'tve been but I was surprised he knew about Slicky.

"Sure." I told him I wasn't little. I was six feet tall by the time I was only twelve. I helped out at Slicky's distillery. Especially during raids. The state troopers'd tell the local cops when there was going to be a raid and the local cops would call Slicky. Slicky'd hire a bunch of us big kids who could handle heavy lifting to help out during raids. We'd sling those twenty-gallon tins into the creek next to the factory and float'em downstream. The specific gravity of alcohol being less than that of water, they'd float right through the middle of Mechanicville. Then we'd get into the back of one of those canvas-covered trucks he had and ride down to the end of the stream with Joyce's hired guns. We'd catch'em all before they reached the Hudson. Most of'em, anyway. We hid one tin under a bush and I had my first drunk on bathtub gin. Twelve years old. My *God* I was sick. I *never* could drink gin after that.

I remember he was quiet for a minute and then he said, "What a different life we had growing up." It was funny. Even though he was older acting now, he still had some of his "younger Harry" nervous habits. He'd twitch and drum his fingers on the dash. I wondered if they were natural or whether he needed time to wind down from acting. He said he was supposed to go off to Europe after his graduation in 'thirty-one, but instead he never got to graduate. Instead he watched everything get stolen from them, and his father just disintegrated. Lost his friends, his money and then, I guess, his mind. Pretty sad, I had to admit. I reminded him a lot of people went broke in the Depression and he bellows at me, "Broke? *Broke? Shit!* A lot of people might have *gone broke*, but my father was robbed! *Robbed*, goddamn it! Robbed! *Every cent.* It *wasn't* the Depression. Christ. We would've weathered that if it hadn't been for him."

Now, that was the old Harry I knew. All piss and vinegar. And I just had to admire that pluck, by the Jesus. Oh, yes. His family could have *weathered* the storm with a measly five mil. Ah. Just weathering the storm. Weathering the old storm.

"Don't know why, there's no sun up in the sky, Stormy Weather . . . ."

I should have said I admired how he and his family could've weathered the storm with only five million. Oh, what courage. I'm out throwing stones at shotgun guards on coal trains so they'll chuck coal back at us, getting hit with massive chunks of coal so I could bring them home to burn in the furnace, but his family could squeak by on five mil? I don't *why* I didn't say that to him. I mean, I wasn't bashful or anything, I . . . I don't know.

Well, hell, I do know. I still wasn't quite believing all this. I think I believed him about his age. No, I did. I did believe him. But, well, he was just such a liar. Oh, God, I don't know what I believed. He was just such a liar. He seemed to be at *that* point, anyways. I wished I'd said something right then. I might have . . . What? What would I have done? What the hell would I have done? What could I do that was different? I mean, here I am, running a store on a shoestring, with a wife and four kids. Jennie wasn't working. Outside the store, I mean. *Damn it!* I swore no wife of mine would ever work. I swore it. No man lets his wife work. No real man. And then she just had to take that clinic job with all of those doctors. We could've pulled out of it, but she was throwing a seven over the bills. Up there at that, that, that clinic. Handling urine samples every day . . . endangering us.

[*There is a long silence.*] I'm not being honest, am I? I am . . . sorry . . . Jane, forgive me. We needed you . . . *I* needed you to work. I *needed* the money. Oh, God, I was in such a mess by 'fifty-nine. I borrowed from everybody in the family. I couldn't get out of this hole I was in and I spent everything. I used all the money Annie had saved for the boys' college. I remember them sitting on the couch and agreeing to it.

And now look. I'm out of money again. In this jackpot. God, Jennie, I just can't believe you've been dead three years this month. Just cannot.

Cannot believe . . . . Three years. July thirty-first, nineteen eighty-four. Just a few weeks from now. The money's just about gone. We spent most of it when you were dying. Annie's stock. Forty thousand dollars. Forty thousand iron men. All gone before you died, Jane . . . . Well, no. All right. I mean, I mortgaged the house before you died. I sold it after you died, Jane. Fifty-three biggies minus the second mortgage. That's gone. All gone. That's a lot of berries, boys and girls. All gone. Gone with the wind. And I really don't give a damn. You always said I could piss through more money than anyone you knew. [*Another long silence.*]

All right. All right. Shut up, George. Crying like some old man. Get back to work. You've got to get back to this, George. You're running out of time! Where am I? Where's that note? Did I make a note? Oh, hell, I don't want to run this thing back. A note, a note! My kingdom for a note. Oh, damn, here it is. Right on the *Times* crossword puzzle. What the hell does "stormy weather" mean?

"Storrrr-meeee weather! Don't know why, there's . . . ."

What *is* "Stormy weather"? *Jesus Christ* what *is* "Stormy weather"?

Oh, yes, yes, yes, yes. Right. *That's* right. He said his family could've weathered the Depression with five mil.

I said I didn't say it to him, but I did. I said all of *Mechanicville* could have weathered the Depression on five million bucks! That is a **lot** of berries. And right then, he stops talking. *Bang!* And goes all quiet. All quiet on the Western Front. We're, oh, a few miles from the Brown Log now and he suddenly pipes up and asks what I was doing in the summer of 'twenty-nine. Outta nowhere. Sometimes he'd sound like Harry the kid and he did now. I . . . I was keeping an eye on this bird. It was, ah, so. . .ah, strange the way he suddenly switched in and out. As if he . . . oh, hell, I don't know. "What was I doing in the summer of 'twenty-nine?" I said. I was going to grade school and just starting my paper route.

He asked me if I remembered what stood out from that summer. Again, an odd question, but I did recall nineteen twenty-nine. I understood why he was asking it. In fact, I remember saying to him, "It was a funny year. It was like the year something ended." I told that by the time I was fourteen, I knew 'twenty-nine was a year where . . ." and I couldn't find the words here and he said it. He had it cold: "Where everything after it would be different forever." Damn, yes. That was it. Perfect. I remember he said it again: "Where everything after it would be different forever."

Did I remember the summer? Like yesterday! Delivering papers at Slicky Joyce's speak and seeing old Doc Purcell shoot up Frankie Osgood every day. Frankie was a legal morphine addict from the war and he'd run up to Doc all crazy and sweating and stick out his arm and say, gruff, like this, "Gotta have it, Doc! Gotta have it." His words came out like a machine gun and he'd be sweating buckets and desperate and he'd point to his arm. "Gotta have it, Doc! Gotta have it." And Doc would stop what he was doing and take out his bag, jab Frankie in the arm and Frankie would sink onto a stool with a big "Ahhhhhhh!"

"You recall that summer vividly?" he asked me. "Vividly." Harry the Elder—that's what I came to call the other Harry in my mind— Harry the Elder had this odd way of speaking. Vividly? Yeah, sure I did. Delivering papers to a whole line of new houses on Dewey Avenue. You know? Backed up against that cemetery where Jane's family's buried? Ah, no. You don't. God, I remember those houses. *Every* one of them was my customer and, within a year, I lost every one of them except one. Every one but one. *One* customer left! And that's because all but *one* house had been repossessed. Most stayed empty for quite a while. It was like delivering on a ghost street.

He was quiet for quite a while. Although, like Harry the Younger, Harry the Elder's limbs moved a lot. A real norvis Orvis, this guy. So, finally, I said, "Hey! You there?"

"Yeah," he says. "I was just thinking how we started out so differently and how within a year we were the same." Whelp, I didn't follow that and said so. He says that that summer he went to off to Europe. He was quiet for a bit and he lets out this long exhale and says, "And I was supposed to go back again right after graduation in 'thirty-one and spend a year—a year!—in Europe. Instead, I watched Father lose everything and just barely avoid prison. It was a nightmare." And then he laughed this funny laugh. Clapped his hands together like he was applauding. Sometimes we react so oddly to a bad memory. Maybe we just have to laugh at them.

"So. . . .?" I say. Well, his father had been a very successful broker on Wall Street, he says, and someone had been stealing the company blind for about five years. "Your godfather?" I ask him. Yes, he says really slowly. He lit up a cigarette and drummed his fingers on the dash. They had some Dorsey Brothers' tune on. I shifted the cigarette I had to my left hand and turned it up a bit. I told him how much my cousin Joe loved them. He bought all the original waxes when they came out. I remember going to Albany with him on the train to buy them.

"Where's he now?" he asked.

Joe went down in the Battle of Leyte in October of 'forty-four. October 25th with the Samuel Roberts. I saw him not long before that. He hadn't heard from his parents in six months. He was working ships stores. Poor bastard. He couldn't even swim. Imagine that. Mother Navy puts a guy who can't even swim on board a destroyer? Joe said to me, "George," he said, "I'm not going to make it."

"What did you tell him?" Harry said.

"Well, even though he was older than me, I was like his older brother. I always defended him. We were both only children."

"Like brothers. I understand." Harry says.

"Joe," I said to him, "Joe, you can't talk that way! You *can't!* You have to believe you're coming back. Believe you're always going to live. Otherwise you die."

"Damn right," he says softly out and claps his hands again, softly though. "Damn right. Otherwise they get you and you always have to get them. I had an old Sarge in my unit. We were coming into Anzio—I went back after a long recoup in England. We were in this LST and this young kid suddenly started saying he wasn't going to make it. And Sarge grabbed the boy and shouts in his face, 'Listen you little cocksucker. You're gonna step off this shitcan and you're gonna kill the first twenty fucking krauts you see, see? And you're gonna *live* through this like the rest of us and you're gonna go home to your mama because she's *waiting* for you, *expecting* you to come home. And you're gonna cut the *balls* off every one of them stinking fucking krauts you kill and you're gonna bring them home to her because *you're* gonna live and **they** *aren't!*' And he's really rolling now, clapping his hands and all.

"Kid went ashore?"

"The world's exploding around us and the kid goes in there like Audie Murphy. Suddenly he's not with us and the Sarge finds him and hauls him off this Jerry and drags him up with us, *screaming* at the kid all the time, 'You hafta kill twenty first *before* you can cut their balls off, you stupid cocksucker!'"

Forgive me. I know my language is terrible. That's how war is. Apparently this sergeant called everybody a cocksucker as a term of endearment. I remember Harry laughing, then he wasn't laughing, then he's laughing again. I wondered if he'd been taking bennies when I wasn't looking. Woof. Boy made me jumpy.

I remember the radio playing another Dorsey just then and how it brought me back to that time when Joe's ship had docked at Pearl City. "My cousin Joe had told me he had this premonition, Harry. Joe said, 'I have this premonition I'm going to die, George.'"

It made me upset and angry—damn, I'm starting to cry just thinking about it—and I told Joe he had to believe he was going to live. He stopped talking like that, but I realized it was for me.

"Did you see him again, George?"

"No. I didn't. He died four months later. I told myself for years that he'd lived and ended up on an island where no one knew him."

"You couldn't protect him forever, George."

I didn't want him to say that. I said I just wanted to think he'd made it—made it to a happier place. Out on an island some place, living with a little native girl. I should've *done something*! I should've done something. . . Aw, hell, Joe. What could I have done? God, Joe.

Oh, go to hell . . . Let me get a beer.

So, where was I? I don't know. I think he said . . . . I don't know. Somehow we got on the topic of Joe's parents. They weren't bad people. They just neglected him when he needed them and then they went to pieces when he died. I think they were angry he'd gone in. They were never the same after. I said I always thought they were both *off* after his death, if he got my meaning."

He did. It was how his father became within a year and then went totally to pieces by 'thirty-three. We drove along for awhile without speaking and then he says, "Sometimes you just can't protect them. You just get revenge for them." I asked if he got revenge. "Oh yes. Yes. Yes, I did." He laughed and then he laughed some more. It made my skin crawl. Then out of the blue he shouts, "Oh, listen! He's playing Paul Whitman," and he hummed that for about a half a minute.

Then he says again, "Yes, I got revenge on my godfather." I thought it was funny that he never called the guy by his name. Always "my godfather." You know? Strange. Like he hated to say the words. The godfather was one bastard of a human being. Bled Dad's company, set up fake corporations and even had a company that did land development in Garden City. Harry said the odd thing was, that *made* money, which was why they moved there. They kept their Oyster Bay house."

I said, "Did your godfather? Move to Garden City, I mean?" Then I asked, "What the hell's his name, anyway? Your godfather." And he says, "Valentine Roosevelt." I laughed out loud. I was pretty sarcastic. "Come on. Roosevelt. Really." He said it was true—some distant relation of the Roosevelts.

No, the godfather didn't move there. He lived in Locust Valley and kept his house there and built another on the south shore. Well, actually— and this is the kick in the groin—he did end up living part of the time in Garden City. Harry said, "He moved in after we moved out in 'thirty-one. He bought it from Dad for ten cents on the dollar. To *help dad* out he said."

"Didn't your father know?"

"All these schemes Uncle Ned had—he was nicknamed for Ned Buntline—all those schemes went along perfectly until the Crash. Didn't affect the company until the Crash and then the company began to unravel. Father kept paying off the company debts as long as he could."

"But didn't your father know?" he always seemed to say "Father," rather than "my father" or "Dad." "*Fawtha*," he'd say. Fawtha this and Fawtha that.

Anyways, Harry was pretty sure Fawtha had suspected from around 'twenty-eight, when things first started to go bad everywhere.

I was watching the road pretty closely now, because there were some hot rods doing tricks in the passing lane on 9 and I didn't wanna get creamed. I wanted to ask him if dear old dad was a bona fide moron, but I think he anticipated I was thinking that way and said, "Father was so . . . he was so . . . good hearted, he couldn't approach Ned. He told me later he just couldn't believe it."

So Ned started spreading the same suspicions about Harry's father. Harry had his lighter out and he was flicking it open and shut as he talked about Ned. Drove me crazy. The hot rodders came up again.

"The market crashed, the business was going under, and *everybody* was looking for somebody to blame." Or something like that. I didn't think the kids wanted to drag with us, so I kept letting them by. And Harry isn't noticing anything. He's just clickin' the Zippo. And droning on, "Uncle Ned's doing what he can to help grease Fawtha's skids." Click, click.

The kids apparently did want to drag. They came up on the side. A souped up Ford roadster—about a twenty-seven Model A I'd say—and a forty-nine Hudson. They roared by while Harry was saying something about Ned buying their Garden City house for ten cents on a dollar and telling everyone he'd actually pulled the business out of bankruptcy." Harry's clicking the frigging lighter at a mile a minute now, absolutely oblivious to the Indy 500 happening outside—vroom!—and going on about Father being *ruined* and everyone blaming him. Click goes the Zippo, the flame a mile high.

They're roaring by at about ninety now, then slowing down, doubling back and doing it again. "He lost his seat on the exchange . . ." click . . . "and spent every last dollar paying off fucking Ned's debts as if they were his own." Click. "The stupid shit." Vroom!

Harry's voice was vicious. "We lost our home in Oyster Bay. Lost all our friends." The Zippo clicking like mad. Everybody believed Ned. Well, you know, get the worst word in first . . . . Meanwhile, click, click, click.

Then **VROOM**. They come one up on each side. I move into the middle lane, like I'm being guided like a liner between two tugs. Harry abruptly stops talking, leans down under the dash, flips a switch and says, "Punch that thing, Georgie!" I hit that gas pedal and it was like it had a *rocket* underneath! We shot away from those two kids as if they were on bicycles.

They were just dropping away and he's back on Ned again. He was obsessive. I had to sidetrack him, "Not everybody believed Ned, right?"

"No, not everyone. When we'd lost the Oyster Bay house, a friend let us live in his beach house for nothing. Then he jumped off One Irving Place." Harry laughed a laugh that wasn't a laugh. "Made a big splash on Broadway."

This was, oh, mid-nineteen-thirty? June. Yes. His whole family ended up living in a trailer, staying in little campsites out on Long Island. He was like a subdued volcano. "In a trailer," he kept saying, just harping on it. "In a trailer," he kept repeating.. "Pretending like we're vacationing. In a miserable . . . rotten . . . stinking . . . little . . . trailer. The four of us, in a trailer."

Well, Mr. Dooley, thank **God** the Brown Log Inn came up suddenly on the right. In a heartbeat—not even—he was saying, "Hey Dad? Let's get that voh-doe-dee-oh-doe stuff offa there and get something cool on." He

punched a button and sighed the words, "Ahhhhhhh. . .Miles. Dee-lish!"
I'm wondering, Miles who?

Harry the Kid—Harry the Younger—was back. Harry the Elder was
gone. It made me feel—I don't feel like a man admitting this—but it made
me feel petrified. He was two people. Two. Brrrrr. Harry snapped the brim
of his hat, flashed me a grin, and said, "And pops? Living in a trailer? Well,
daddio, let's just say, it's definitely not in the groove. And this cat, he made
sure someone paid large for that when the time came."

Like a jackrabbit, he hopped out just as I was parking, adjusted his look
in the mirror then reached under the seat, popped open a drawer that
looked like it couldn't've been there a second before and grabbed a small
cloth bag. His voice was like, his voice was like—sorry, can't stop this
coughing—like a kid's voice. Christ. I could *not* believe it. I can hear him!
"Got a chick inside waitin' on sump'in sparklin', Georgie, and I *don't* mean
champagne! Hey-*hey*!" He shook the bag with his left hand and it made a
muffled, rattling noise. Diamonds.

So Harry's the Elder's gone and Harry the Younger's bouncing into the
Brown Log Inn. Jekyll and Hyde. If I'd known just how much Jekyll and
Hyde, I would've driven off right then—taken my chances. But, hell, no.
Not George. George always has to stay just a little longer. Just a little bit
longer. Always taking it to the edge. God all Jesus. . . God all Jesus, I took it
to an edge I never wanted to see. If I could ever turn back the clock . . . .

CHAPTER 9

Okay. I'm back. Tape running? Let's see, uh, yup. Little wheels turning? Yup. Mine are, too. Okay. So, we're, um, we're at the Brown Log Inn. I sat in the car wishing to Christ I could have a beer like the one I'm having right now. Lovely. I had the windows down and could hear the music coming out the front door—some kind of combo playing country western. I grabbed a kid and had him buy me a few beers. I decided I'd find out what else he had in that car. I mean, what else he had hidden in that car. Jesus, what a car it was. Soft leather seats, beautiful interior. He even had walnut in there, where'd you'd normally expect just to have a flat metal dash. Not like now where everything's plastic. This car had the real goods.

He'd gone deep into the bar, so I was thorough—found a flashlight built into the glove compartment and got down to work. He had drawers all *over* the place—jewelers tools and stones and soft little cloth bags. Like a fool I'd left the radio on, but now that I knew it couldn't run down that bank of batteries he had, I switched over to a station in Albany with something other than that squeak and squawk he had on. I got ahold of something on the bottom of the driver's seat and gave it a tug. A drawer slid out and in it were two .45 automatics, identical to my service issue. I stuffed one down in my pants.

At that moment I was actually down with my body almost under the wheel, when I heard, "Hey, Jah-gee! What'd'yah doing, pally?" I thought to myself, "Oh, shit. What do I do now?" I had the beer and I poured a little on the floor and grabbed an empty jeweler's bag and rubbed it in it. I slid the drawer in and came up holding the beer bottle and the bag in my hand, like this. "I think I mighta gotten a little beer on the rug."

He bellows, "Jesus Christ, Georgie. Not beer! Christ. That frigging . . . sorry. That rug's hard to clean, Dad." Then he laughed and said to the girl with him—did I say he had two girls with him?—and he says, "Old geezers . . . ." She laughed, but obviously didn't think it was all that funny. She was cute. Bobbed hair. Pert little nose, buck teeth. Like Dorothy Collins on *The Hit Parade.* Hubba hubba. How I love a buck-toothed woman! She looked like Jennie. She was clutching the bag with the stones in it and jiggling it up and down.

He said she was Jeannie and that gave me a start! You can imagine. Harry says, "And this is Stephanie." I actually hadn't seen the other woman's face. She stepped up and shook my hand. Believe that? Stuck her hand into the car and shook it? Jesus . . . Skiddies. I told her to wait a minute and I stepped out and shook it again. Christ, she was tall and dark. And *luscious*? Oh, my God. You don't know the half of it. Well, goddamn if Tall, Dark and Luscious didn't actually look me up and down. Oh, God. As Joe Keyes used to say, she'd give a man an erection so large and so hard, a beaver could gnaw on the end with no visible effect. Had long hair, like Veronica Lake, except brunette, and features like Jinx Falkenburgh.

You know, I was in a photo shoot with Jinx Falkenburgh in Chicago in 'forty-two. Yours truly and the two other Kings I bunked with at midshipman school. Let me get another beer . . .

Okay, so Harry shoots an arm around Tall, Dark and Luscious, jams his head in the car window and says, "Hey! That a quarter on the floor?" I went over, looked in and he says, "Naw. Must be leftover beer. I thought it was a *quarter* on the floor." Real emphasis on the word "quarter." He's turning to me so his face is hidden from the girls, and winks as he's says "quarter on the floor" again. Oh . . . my . . . Lord! Tall, Dark and Luscious is the Congress Street Skiddie who can pick up the *coins!* I had to get a grip before I could look at her again. She smiled like she knew the answer to a thousand riddles.

"Come on inside for a beer, Georgie," he says. Now, I'm *really* frightened waiting out in the parking lot where somebody might see me, but I'm even **more** frightened with the thought of going into that bar. I pull him away from the girls and say, "What kind of jamoke you think I am? What if somebody knows me in there?"

"So? So?" Really snotty. I wanted to give him the flat of my hand against the side of his head. So, I'm thirty-five, I say, with four kids. What am I doing here?

And he gives me this wise-ass look, and he's moving, you know, everything moving on'im, and he snaps the brim on his hat and looks away and then looks back and says, "You're here drinking. You're getting drunk'n telling lies, same as you're doing every night in your shithole little town. C'mon, Jah-gee. What is this? Fairytale time? You drink. I drink." He looks over his shoulder and looks back. "The girls drink. Nobody's gonna say anything." And he pauses and says, "But everyone'll know where you were, *when* . . . you know?—things happened? If oo-yay, et-gay my ift-dray? Yeah, dad. There you go." And he whispers so only I can hear, "Hey, hey! It's alibi time. Let's go get that drink, baby, and make eye contact."

He grabs Dorothy Collins and heads off. I'm shaking—embarrassing to admit—but I am shaking. So, I concentrate on Tall, Dark and Luscious. How it is she can do what she does with what she has? I try to keep my face straight going in. And I'm wishing she wouldn't take my arm because, first of all, I'm married, and second of all, it feels good. And third of all, it feels good. Dangerous thoughts. Made me think of being on the Main Island and going to see the Princess Papouli and her girls in Honolulu. Oh, Jesus. Those Hawaiian women. At fourteen, or fifteen, they had these beautiful tummies and breasts so erect you thought they were carved out of India rubber. Nobody ever believes me when I say we just went over to eat and watch'em dance. Sometimes I can't believe myself.

So we get inside and the place is hopping. God almighty, just jumping! I can't buy a drink. Junior's throwing money at the bartender, who's looking at him with that sophisticated adoration only bartenders can achieve. God, I just called him Junior, didn't I? I called him Junior in the bar, too. It, ah, it . . . it felt natural. Made it better, too. You know, I'm standing here with this guy who's supposed to be so much younger'n me. Simply eerie how he just turned it on'n'off.

[*This part is garbled by damaged tape.*] . . . band's, I don't know, seven, eight [*pieces*] . . . electric guitars and they're ripping into Western Swing. The bandleader . . .ade Cooley . . . by [*H*]ank Williams! . . . and next thing, Dorothy Collins is [*waving?*] frantically at the guy and she yells out in this girlish falsetto, "Yoo-hoo! Steel? *Steel!!* Over here! Billy? Hi Billy! Hi!" The bandleader waves and the band goes into *Jambalaya* and Dorothy's in *seventh* heaven. She's kissing her jewel bag. Honestly.

Junior's real low-key. Again, it's that blending in with the woodwork yet being seen enough to be remembered routine. I said he had sunglasses on, didn't I? Aviator glasses. Looked like your average kid with sunglasses. Who'd ever know his eyes were green like mine?

He nudges me, points over to a woman who was easily, hell, in her mid-seventies. He waves and she looks over, waves back. "Jane Blynn," he says. "Owns the place? Seventy-five. Amazing. Wave to Jane." I wave. The old lady waves. I mean, old for then. She seemed ancient then. God. She'd be seven years older than I am right now. And I'm not even going to make seventy-five. I'm . . I'm not ready to die . . . and then, I am ready to die. Oh, God, stay with me.

Um . . . so, I'm on my toes. I'm nervous. Man. Nervous in the service. Not as much as later. God, *no!* And I'm thinking more about why I am there. "Why?" I'm asking myself. "Money, stupid," myself says to me. The band's stomping, crowd's jammed together jitterbugging. It was deafening. I remember Harry shouting something like, "Hair scoopin' it up, Jah-gee!" but actually it was "They're whoopin' it up, Jah-gee!" And out of nowhere I said to him, "A bunch of the boys were whoopin' it up in one of them Yukon halls, while the fellow at the player piano was stealthily scratching his balls." Well, he starts to laugh and so does Tall, Dark and Luscious, who I hadn't realized had been listening, because I thought she was prattling on with Dorothy Collins. I felt a bit self-conscious for a second, but Tall Dark isn't fazed at all and when the song suddenly changes to "Heart of My Heart," she says she wants to dance. Harry starts swearing about the song and floats off somewhere with Dorothy and I could kill him. All I want to do is *get* the hell out and *get* on the road and *get* the job done.

I tell Tall Dark I don't want to dance and kill another beer. Because the place is jammed, we're standing close—close enough to hear, but too close really—and she asks me if I ran MacFinn's. Thank God she said it when she did, because part of the crowd is really drunk and they are trying to sing along with "Heart of My Heart."

Oh, swell. I'm thinking. This is just peachy keen—just what I feared the most. I told her I did. She used to come in all of the time for our perfume selection. It went to hell after I left. I said I was sorry. Then she says, "A lot of things went to hell after you left. I had a friend at the track who used get 'colorful things' from you. Blues and reds. And things to help us go up and down."

I told her that her remark ruined her chances for Campfire Girl of the Year award. Stupid me, I asked her if it was to help her *friend* or *her* to go up and down? She got her face just inches from mine—phew!—and I will always remember her saying, "Sometimes a girl likes to go up and sometimes a girl likes to go down. Up and down. And up . . . and down. And *up* . . . and *down.*" She moved her tongue to illustrate, shall we say, what she meant. It was pretty obvious she wasn't talking about the merry-go-round ride at Kaydeross Park.

My heart was already racing and now it's pounding. I'm no saint, but I wasn't about to cheat on my wife. Tall Dark asks me to dance again and I tell her I think I should be leaving and, just then—I mean, I barely got the frigging word "leaving" out—a voice behind me says, "Maybe you should let Daddy go home. Maybe the old man should leave *little* girls alone."

The voice was near, like the guy was on my shoulder. I felt a hundred and ten and start to get angry, when I saw him. Oh, Oh, Mother *McCree!* A shitkicker. And a *real* Junior, twenty-four, -five, not an imitation Junior. And huge—he looked like he'd just milked a hundred cows and then eaten the herd for a snack. Raw. Life Lesson number 527: go to a shitkicker bar, expect to see shitkickers. This was . . . one . . . big . . . shitkicker! A Neanderth . . . .

[The tape is badly damaged here and throughout about the next five minutes. George seems to state that he tried to ignore the large man, but the man was very drunk, wanted to fight and was looking for any excuse.] Neanderthal Boy couldn'ta cared less if it'd been Tall Dark or a statue in downtown Manila. It looked like a woman. It was a good excuse . . . [*"to fight." It seems as if George sought to leave quietly with the woman, that in his youth he loved scrapping and probably would have egged the man on, but he had changed since the war. He continues:]* . . . looking around for Harry and Dorothy, who have evidently taken off their bandages and are pulling the Claude Rains routine on me, and as I'm turning back, Tall Dark is throwing a drink in Neanderthal Boy's face. Oh, dear Jesus! As I'm ducking the liquid, I'm watching Jane Blynn motioning the group's leader to pick up the sound and the tempo—which he does and all hell br . . . .

[The next intelligible part finds them in the parking lot for reasons that are obvious.] Neanderthal Boy has his meat hooks in Tall Dark . . . and, like I said, she's in pain . . . sonuvabitch could run . . . ahead of him. Suddenly there's this screech of tires and a car is barrel-assing right at us and everything starts goes into slow motion. Like when we were hit by that Zero. A split second and then it's pandemonium. Ten shells ripped the deck in a, in a, in a *fraction* of a second! And then, suddenly there's this *slowness*—I don't know what to call it, but it's from your adrenalin—and *you're* moving at top speed, but the shells are suddenly, suddenly they're, they're, going into the deck, not slowly, but as if you can see them rip into it, one at a time. Kah-*chunk!* *Thunk! Thunk!* Unh! Oh! Oh! Jesus! My chest! I begin to jump away and Neander is just *standing* there like a deer in the headlights, mouth wide open, clenching her arm, kinda holding it up in the air. But, but she's just standing there watching—watching the car coming at'em—just as, I don't know, calm with her other hand holding up the collar on her coat, like she's

modeling it. And I'm *screaming . . . unh, unh . . . screaming* "GET OUTTA THE FRIGGIN' WAY, GET OUT! *GET OUT!*"

And she, she just steps back a step, just step a little backward. I grabbed her and the car went into Neanderthal Boy and I thought, "Okey dokey. Here we go. Front page headline of *The Saratogian*: 'Vehicular manslaughter.'" But Neanderthal Boy? Something's finally clicked in and the bastard's already pushing himself *off and away* from the *Studebaker* and rolling on the gravel for about ten feet. Christ!

Terrible reactions on that guy. Wouldn't've wanted that simpleton with me under fire. Never could've followed an order. I would've had to shoot him in the leg. I had to with one seaman. Wouldn't move. Just froze. So many served who never should've been there.

Well, Neanderthal Boy may have been a frontal lobe short, but I was on! Every, *every,* nerve, alive! Lord, Jesus, I haven't felt like this since, Christ, the war! I see *every*thing! I hear *every*thing! *Everything! Everything* that's happening! The sound of the car brakes. Gravel crunching. The look on her face—like the Sphinx. I'm hepped up and it's not subsiding. Doors swing open on both sides as the Studebaker's coming to a stop. Dorothy's opening a rear door and I'm shoving Tall Dark in. I look over and Harry's throwing *open* the driver's door and he's got a gun. I'm thinking, "Oh, Jiggly J. Joy. Forget *The Saratogian!* This is front page *Daily News!* Murder One!"

I . . . I, I scramble like a kid through the front seat. Hey! Second time in a night. Practice makes perfect! Neander's still on the ground and I'm up on Harry before he can shoot him. I'm, I'm positive he was going to. No one was around us—pretty sure—but I'm absolutely sure the boy's seen Harry's .45 because he's trying to hide his face. Waiting to be shot, I guess. Smart enough to do that. I whispered into Harry's ear, "Don't, Harry. Don't. He's just a moron, Harry. C'mon. C'mon. Before he looks up and really sees your face. Let's shove off." He let me lead him back on a run and I get him through to the passenger side, he shouts at me to go easy on his arm and we are off like a shot.

It's funny? You know, now that I think of it, I'm sure . . . I know for certain . . . more was going on around us. I know the music was loud and people were shouting and things were happening all round us, but that's all I can see in my mind's eye. I got us out onto Route 9 and heard what I thought was a sobbing or choking in the back and figured either Tall Dark or Dorothy was crying. Maybe both. Then I see Tall Dark in the rearview lighting up two smokes at once. Calm? Like Lauren Bacall. Looks me right in the eyes and passes me a smoke. *Cool* as a cucumber. I hear the sobbing again and it's Dorothy Collins laughing! And saying in this silly, breathless Marilyn Monroe voice, "Hah-ree! Hah-ree! That was ***ex-ci-ting!***"

And I reached my hand across the front seat and gently slid it over the .45 in his hand before he could lift it.

CHAPTER 10

Harry wasn't quiet very long, but I could see what he was doing, so I turned the radio on to get Harry the Younger's music. It came up and he started to twitch and move and snap his fingers and was humming a little. And, bingo! Harry the Younger's back with us. He turns around in the seat so he can look at Dorothy and I remember his eyes met mine. I don't know who he was, but he wasn't who he was a minute before. He says to her in this annoyed but not too annoyed voice, "Hey, Jeannie?"

"Yeah, Harry?" she says in this Marilyn Monroe voice. "Yeah, Harry?"

Oh, was she stupid. Beautiful? Oh, baby. If ignorance truly was bliss, then she laughed in her sleep.

He says to her something like, maybe from now on he could meet her at some place quiet? I recall so well his saying, "Can't see what a class chick like *you* sees in a place like the Brown Log Inn." And then *he* laughs.

It was later that I remembered her saying, "Yeah, but Harry, it wasn't my . . . . Yeah. Sure, Harry. Sure." Later I thought that was odd. It wasn't her what? But, big mouth me, right then I jumped in and said Skiddies like to take square dance lessons there from live hillbillies.

But he's on her side now: "Aw, dad. Give the girl a break. What're we gonna do with these *old* fogies, huh?" Tall Dark lit another smoke for herself. I looked in the rearview and she looked me right in the eyes again. There was enough in that look to say to me what she'd do with this old fogey. Phew . . . . baby.

"Hey, girls!" he says, "stretch out your hands," and dumps something in Dorothy's. "C'mon, you, too, Stephanie." Tall Dark's hand comes over and I can hear the clicking of the stones. And, oh, how I can remember him snapping his fingers and laughing, "Hey, hey! Sah-ry for the bad entertainment. Can we forget all about this?" And they all laughed together and Dorothy and Tall Dark said they certainly could. Oh, sure. Tee-hee-hee-hee. They're all laughing, but I know he wants to wring Dorothy's neck like a chicken's. He didn't offer me any stones, by the way.

We drove a little further and dropped them off at another spot. I can't remember where now, but Tall Dark said she has her car there. I'm thinking to myself that I'm glad it wasn't anywhere near Skidmore, because I sure as hell didn't wanna go anywhere near where old eagle eyes Annie was. But what I really should have been doing is asking myself what a couple of Skiddies are doing here before school starts. Jesus. Frankly, I was rattled. I mean, Tall Dark had lit us one last smoke and as she handed it to me over the back of the seat, she ran a wet finger down the back of my neck as she got out. Aw Jesus. *She* knew what we should be doing. But, like I said, instead of me asking the smart boy questions I should've been asking myself, all I'm really doing is thinking to myself, "George, what are you doing here?" We took off again.

I was calmer now and I was petrified and I do remember yelling at him, "What the hell were you doing back there?" "Holy Christ, Harry. You try to run some guy over in a parking lot. And what's with the .45?" We were near the city limits and I was really nervous. I looked over at and I screamed at'im, "You were gonna kill him!" Bastard tells me to keep my eyes on the road. Said I was dreaming. I'm dreaming? No way, buster. *I* wasn't dreaming. *He* was dreaming if he thought I was staying in. I told him I wanted out. *Out!* And on the double, mister!

I remember like a minute ago the sonofabitch asking me in this calm voice—a voice that made me even more edgy—if I'm angling for more money. "Jesus Christ," I'm yelling at him. "*I'm not angling for anything!* This is crazy! You understand me? Crazy. *Nuts!*" I was screaming and pounding on the wheel. Christ, how the hell'd I ever let him talk me into this? I tell him, "I'm pulling over. You take it from here."

Just between us girls? I *had* to pull over. I was shaking so badly! I swung into—oh, I can't think of the name of it. You know, that motor court just above the Wishing Well? And he was all calm. "No, George," he says very calmly. His voice was level and, and it was dangerous. " I don't think so, George." Very, very calmly. I hate it when a man repeats your name like that. It's never good.

I hit the brakes, jammed it into neutral and said I'd hitchhike back if I had to—and screw his fuckin'arm, because if that was the only excuse he was using, I didn't give a steaming pile of shit. I make like I'm shifting and actually am reaching for the gun. God, I don't know what the hell I thought I'd do with it. Point it at him and scare him, I guess. I don't know. I was younger then and still so close to it all.

I slid my hand softly over the seat, but Mr. Calm, Cool and Collected says, "I've got the gun, Georgie." Oh, God. I couldn't believe that I'd set that back on the seat after I'd lifted it out of his hand. Son...of...a...bitch. It'd been quite a while since anyone'd fired anything at me and *that* wasn't at close range in a car. I thought to myself, "Pretty stupid, George." I don't mind admitting that I thought I might soil my knickers. "Well, George old boy," I'm thinking, "if this is it, you might as well pop the question." So I ask him straight out if he intends to shoot me. "I don't *do* that stuff, George!" and says he *told* me that before. He has it to protect himself from me. *Me!* He asks me if I get it.

I get it, I tell'im. What was he getting ready to do with the .45 in the parking lot? Help Neander pick his nose with it? My heart was still pounding, but I was getting myself under control. He wasn't gonna shoot me here in front of a little motor court cabin where Sammy Joblots was getting his rocks off with some dolly other than Mrs. Joblots. But the bastard's two jumps ahead of me. No, he's smarter than that, he says. He doesn't have to shoot me, because I've been seen. The girls saw me.

Lord, God, what a horse's ass I was. "So it's a frame, Harry." He says no. It's just a coincidence. Just worked out as a frame. I laughed in the bastard's face. He got annoyed. He'd been sounding a bit Harry the Younger, but now he's definitely Harry the Elder. And he sticks his jaw out and jams a cigarette in his teeth and says in his FDR voice, "We seize life's gifts. We just have to know what's the gift and what's the booby prize. I received both with Eleanaw."

Oh Jiggly J. Joy. Guy's got a .45 on me and decides to audition for the Bob Hope of the sociopath set. Well, I figured I had nothing to lose. I tell'im either I'm gonna die from the humor or a gunshot wound, but it wasn't any coincidence. "Harry, I figure Dorothy Collins—Jeannie—maybe she's the straight goods. But Tall Dark and Luscious a nice coincidence? Don't make me puke. That Skiddie's a *convenience* not a coincidence. *If* she's a Skiddie."

He was not saying anything, but he's watching me. I just wish I knew if he has the .45 pointed straight at me. This was nuts and getting nuttier. I figured he used Tall Dark to get his diamond customers. Ditzy young girls with too much pin money, so many little rich bitches at Skidmore. Well, no, not all of'em. Corky wasn't that way. Corky was the real thing. Tops.

I asked him how frigging stupid he thought I was.

Sorry 'bout the coughing again. Jesus, this is killing me. Well, that was stupid. It *is* killing me. God, I'm going to die alone. Where the hell is my family now? Where is my life?

All right, let's not get into that. Anyway, I said to him, "You're down on Congress Street where you *'just happened'* to see Stephanie taking up a special 'collection' for the March of Dimes, and it's a 'nice coincidence' she shows up tonight? Oh, yessiree, Bob."

That bebop crap was on. I'd had enough and punched a button to get something else. "Heart of My Heart" came up and suddenly he was not the Calm Boy anymore and started swearing a blue streak. He punched the buttons so hard that nothing is coming up. I reached over and said, "Relax, Robespierre," and hit a button squarely. "Cement Mixer" comes on and we laughed and both said "puttee puttee" at the same time. Funny what you recall.

That broke the tension. I asked what was with that song and he goes as silent as a tomb. I am thinking he is definitely nuttier than grandma's fruitcake at Christmas. And now he's silent, for too long. So yours truly, Mr. Blabbermouth, has to say something and I ask him, "What could the girls do? To me, I mean?"

He said he'd set the place alight, but the girls would say I drove off in the Studebaker. I swear it sounded almost like, almost like he was regretful. It was all coming home now. I'd been an asshole—perfectly round—but didn't realize to what degree. I mean this boy was Churchill's enigma wrapped in a riddle. I said something like, "It's all a frame." He says *I'm* not listening. A spontaneous frame, yes, but not premeditated. That's what he said, "not premeditated."

I told him that made me feel all warm and giggly inside, thank you. He didn't answer. He didn't have to. He had the *gun*! But George can't shut up, a regular Gabby Hayes. Nerves. Both girls can't be in on it, I'm saying. So Jeannie could testify for me. He didn't have anything on her. He was quiet for quite some time and then all he said was— and oh, God, I shall never, ever forget this—he said, "Not yet."

I'm telling you this, because, well, it all just turned right there. I can see that now. I can see I made the decision right then, even though I didn't realize it at that moment. Right at that point is where things just went for the worst. That night everything turned for the worst right at that moment. All I said to him was, "Your life is just filled with lies, isn't it, Harry?" And, as God is my witness—hand to God, may I die right here if I am lying—the song playing on the car radio is "Little White Lies." I mean that's real life. You just can't make this sort of stuff up. You know? If you did, they'd call you Chuck Dickens.

I just sat there, not knowing what to do. The song played through. We both just sat there with the engine running, both smoking. I felt sick. Trapped. I didn't know what to do. Part of me just wanted to run and say, "Try something, Harry. Go ahead." And another part of me said, "You're screwed, George. Oh, you're so screwed." Stuck in another jackpot—*another* jackpot like now. Oh, God what am I going to do? Christ, I hope I'm dead before . . . .

[*Those comments are edited out. They ran to the tape's end. Then a new tape starts. Clinking noises. Sound of liquid pouring in a glass and of drinking.*]

Jesus, I love old age, goddamn piping all screwed up, can't even take a leak like a man anymore.

Okay, where were we? Damn, didn't put down a word. Let's see . . . let's see. Somewhere around the Wishing Well . . . oh, yeah. Yep. Right. I remember sitting through "Little White Lies" wondering if I could get back on the road and ram the Studebaker into a tree at fifty, sixty miles an hour. You know, I was at the wheel. I'd stand a chance. He was in the death seat. Hell, one night in 'fifty-one I jammed our Studebaker right between two trees on Union Avenue near Mike and Joe's Bar and walked away from it! Walked home! I was, shall we say, a little "mellow"? Cops ignored then. Now there's all this DWI stuff like I had in 'seventy-seven. What a year.

Anyways, I walked home. Next morning, Jennie and I took a cab over. The cabbie's *running* on about this jerk who slammed his car in between two big trees on Union? Hah, hah, hah. And then I tell him where we're going. Jesus, was Jane angry! Oh, God! She was so pretty when she was like that . . . . Sixty-five when she died. She was going to learn how to fly a jet at eighty-three. Never made it, did you, honey? Sixty-five, God? I don't understand how all this works.

Anyways, I decided I wasn't drunk enough to crack the car up and survive. Finally I said, "You're always a few steps ahead of me, aren't you?" Wish I'd *really* thought about that when I said it. Maybe I would've understood what the hell was really happening that night. Maybe?

And he said, "No. It's just a matter of *carpe diem*." I didn't reply and he repeated himself: "I said it's just a matter *carpe diem*, you know? Seize the day? It's Latin. You know?" Oh, that really ticked me off. "I know it's Latin, you boob. I took it in high school . . . in college along with the German I took?"

He called me, Mr. Touchy. I called him a *Scheisskopf,* which is German for shithead. I'd spent five years at Union studying German. The "language of science" my profs called it. Then the krauts lose the war and it's never used again. Not only that, five years of German and Uncle Sammy sends me to fight Japs. Your tax dollars at work.

Anyway, I'm angry and he wants to calm me down. Probably figuring that, if I feel too boxed in, I might try to kill him and we'll both end up dying. I did feel trapped, but it wasn't my intention to kill anyone. Lord, God, believe me.

So he's trying to sweet talk me with a bit of logic. When Neanderthal Boy had latched on to me, Harry said so many people saw *me* he figured it was a perfect moment and snuck out the back door with Jeannie. I told he'd left me with one of the Jukes family drooling on my sleeve and, Christ, that made him laugh, which made me angrier. He kept saying, over'n'over, "the Jukes family, the Jukes family, the Jukes family." It was funny, I guess, but I told him to stow it. All I thought about was how I'd get even. I think The Man Upstairs took me too much to heart.

So what was I going to do? I knew he wasn't bluffing. I couldn't go home until we did the job. Everything that night turned on that moment. Everything after that night was never the same again. Never ever again. And so horrible. Oh, my God forgive, forgive me, forgive me. . . .

CHAPTER 11

Sorry about getting so upset. I'm such an old man now. Blubber at everything. So, there I was. I was in. But I told'im I was going to take a very active part in this and I turned to him, looked at him and said, "And you're going to pay my debts, because, whoever wants the Piping Rock *torched* has big reasons and your weeping and wailing about getting killed tells me you need me right now, Chief Broken Wing."

There was a long silence after that. Long. We headed down 9 again. And then—you forget things like this—then out of the dark I hear, "Enough for you to pay back Uncle Jim?"

You know, it's strange what happens with shock and fear. Someone says something you'd never want to hear. When you do hear it, you almost hear it as if—what? Like you're a stranger to the words? Then, they click in and the shock's electric, like that fear that runs over you when you're under fire. I said he didn't know what the hell he was talking about.

I wasn't sure how much he knew, but he knew. He said he heard things. He kept saying, "The way I hear it." The way he hears it, the state's working on indicting Jim and I just happen to leave town to buy this little drugstore in Fort Edward. The way he hears it, I took a lot of drugs, worth about ten grand. The way he hears it, Jim had sent a couple of suits up to Fort Edward to get money. I told him that was bullshit. He says, "That's the way *I* hear it." The way he hears it, when the suits couldn't get the money, they started taking stuff right off the shelves. I told him that was bullshit as well. "That's the way I hear it," he keeps saying—very annoying way of punctuating a sentence. And Mr. Punctuation says, "The way I hear it, somehow you talked them out of it. That's what I hear."

Cute. I'm feeling like I'm going to toss my cookies all over his shiny car. He seemed to know a lot, but I didn't know what he was guessing at. I told him he listened to a lot of fairy stories. He said we all did in life, but this was a story told by someone who knows.

I remember trying to make my voice strong when I asked him who. And he didn't say anything. And I asked, "Uncle Jim?" And he didn't say anything. And I turned on the overhead and looked at him. We're roaring down Route 9 at sixty miles an hour and I turned my head and looked right at him and asked, "Uncle Jim?"

And he still didn't say anything, but he lowered his eyelids so they're almost closed, kind of fluttering shut, like before. I looked back at the windshield. I could see my own reflection in the glass and I gripped the wheel harder. I watched myself say, "At this point it doesn't matter what *I* say. If whoever told you that says I did it, then that's the only story you'll listen to, right?"

I glanced over and he just looked down at his hands. Then he says, real business like, "We'll call this job even. I'll fix it so the whole problem's gone. But because you're helping me out in a pinch, I'll still give you that grand for your troubles."

You know, I should've been happy. Hell, I should've been *relieved*. But I was burning inside. Fuming. I was shouting, "That son of a bitch Leary always wins. The big shot lawyer always wins. He owns the Republican Party. He owns Saratoga County. He owns me. He owns you. **He** sent you here. Yeah. Yeah. This is all a big frame. I am *so* stupid."

He says, "This isn't about you and Leary, stupid. This isn't about Leary. You think everything's about *you*? It's about me. It's about what they need to have me do with the Piping Rock."

They who?

He tried to say he didn't hear it firsthand from Leary. Just from somebody else. I was so angry, so goddamn angry. I just ranted. I, oh God, I ran on, saying things, like, "I ran his store. I ran MacFinn's well—made him money. Leary said he'd pay me. He had me give a lot of *help* to folks at the track. He said he'd pay me." I just went on and on—you know? Saying I'd made a lot of money for Uncle Jim? But he didn't pay me like he said he would. I took care of people he wanted taken care of. It was true. I did. Vets and trainers who needed to be sure that those injured horses could still run. Give the ponies a little, um, "help" getting across the finish line? And I took care of Uncle Jim's summer friends. Their wives need picker-uppers or calmer-downers? Done! I made a lot of money for him. He paid me a good salary . . . but he didn't pay me what he said he was going to. I left E. R. Squibb to work for him because I needed the money. I hated to leave! I sold penicillin to every cough house from MacGregor to Raybrook. I was producing! Jennie begged me not to leave. Uncle Jim offered a lot more.

I yelled at him, "What did you know Harry? I covered for that bastard. He had the gaming money from Piping Rock being counted in the cellar, in the goddamn *cellar*, of MacFinn's so they won't lose a lot if they were raided and Leary's spreading this *crap* around town about what I did? I didn't ask him to do that, did I? I could've lost my license! It was a joke, anyway! Who the hell ever raided the Piping Rock or any of those clubs? Rox? Ahearn? Hathorn? Gaffney? Christ Jesus, not one of'em ever raided any club, even once. Oh! Wait! Maybe Doc Leonard came in and placed them all under citizen's arrest.

Well in the middle of my sixty mile an hour rant, he says, very softly, "Don't be a child. Ahearn shut down Piping Rock in 'thirty-five.'"

Well, that set me off even more. "Gee whiz. And after that, what? What? Nothing. *Nothing!* And who was always at MacFinn's until twelve or one or whenever *they* needed to be downcellar counting Piping Rock money? Huh? Huh? Ahearn? Rox? Was it? *No! No, goddamn it, no! It's me! Me!* The little old latch keeper, you sniveling little shit."

Boy, that hit him. He starts screaming that it's not about me and I scream back, "Who was threatened with a subpoena from the Kefauver Committee? *Me!*"

"Leary was named in the Kefauver Report, Rox, Ahearn . . . ."

"Big *goddamn* deal, Harry. Leary'n'the others are in the Kefauver Report? *Big goddamn deal!* Of course Leary's in the Kefauver Report. He's a mob attorney *and* head of the Republican machine in Saratoga County! And whatever happened to him? Whatever happened to *him? What?* Nothing. That's whatever happened to him! *Nothing! Absolutely nothing!*

"Leary got indicted by the state two years ago," he says in this "here's another card on the deck" voice.

I'm screaming now. "Same thing! Leary's indicted by the state. *Big goddamn deal!* Nothing happened to him then, either. Nothing. *Nothing, nothing, nothing, nothing!* Nothing ever does. Nothing happened to him in 'forty-two. Nothing happens now. Lansky gets three months and Leary? Nothing. Goddamn fucking bastard! Nothing ever does. His lead witness "*mysteriously*" disappears and he's acquitted. One of the holy mysteries. The cops can't find a lousy TV repair man. TV repair man, my ass. He fronted for Leary just like the rest of us."

He's trying to get me to calm down and I am yelling. "And how about after the Kefauver Committee, who gets threatened with a subpoena from the state? Right! Good old George again. He paid me to leave in fifty-two— *paid* me. But he said there'd be more and there wasn't. Uncle Jim could afford to pay. He had millions. Shit. What that bastard promised to pay me he could've found in his couch cushions."

Hyah, hyah, hyah, hyah….. Oh Christ. Oh, God, Harry. Hyah, hyah, hyah, hyah….. Oh, God. It's so funny. The best part is Leary left it all to his niece and she willed it all to the Pope! Not St. Peters Church. *Not* even the Albany diocese. Oh, no, to the friggin' Pope. That's too hilari . . . ! [*There is a long period of coughing.*]

Sorry. I get coughing when I get excited. Got get myself under control. Hang on . . . . Okay. So, it's quiet for a minute and then he says, "Got all that out of your system now, about Leary?" I was really uncomfortable. I said, yes, I did. "George, I don't care about Leary. George, I don't care about *you* and Leary. This isn't about you. This isn't about Leary. In fact" and here he gives this pregnant pause, "I was just playing with you a bit. Havin' a little fun. But, thanks for the info." He laughed like someone who'd just cracked you on the ass with a wet towel in the locker room.

At that point I could have shot him to death I was so angry. I started to say something and he just rolled right on: "I've got a job I've *got* to do for some people. You're in, right?"

Well, that was so embarrassing. I had myself a little temper tantrum and he couldn't've cared less about it all. He just liked using stuff against me. I hated him for it. He knew and I knew he had me by the short hairs. I was silent for a minute, and then I said, "I'm in. What the hell else can I do?" He didn't reply.

He points to me to stay on Roo-nine . . . sorry, Route 9, I mean. We're following the main route into the city? Yes, he says. Oh, sure thing, I say. Let's go down to the police station, ask them to give us an escort and lend us some matches. He got really haughty, said with my degree *I* should know better. **HE** doesn't use matches. I asked the stuck-up Harvard bastard if he wanted me to apologize for my degree.

"Hey, I'm jealous, George. Okay? You made it through school. I didn't. I ended up supporting my parents."

"Oh, boo-hoo—you grew up a rich WASP!" Bastard turned the radio on to drown me out. But I really was just talking to distract myself. I was so behind the eight ball. Here I am being blackmailed into helping this guy torch Piping Rock—the Piping Rock of all places!—and I don't really know why we're doing it. It's not making sense. A defunct nightclub and he's scared to death about not getting the job done? He brings up my old boss but then says it isn't about him? Harry's got to do this job for "them"? Them who? What was wrong with this picture? I thought if I could get him to talk somehow, I might understand. So, I changed the subject and asked how long he'd been doing this. Harry let out this big sigh, like this . . . .

God! Sorry 'bout that. Damn cough. Here, turpenhydrate and codeine—this'll do the trick. I could drink a hundred of these. Jesus! Oh, my chest! God keep me alive.

Where was I? Notepad. Notepad. Where's the pad. *Jesus*, where's the pad? Okay. Here. So—get my glasses—so, then he says that he's been doing this since nineteen thirty-one. *Twenty-three years!* Jesus H. Christ. He'd gone to Chicago in 'thirty-one to try to get a job with a relation of Dad's, but . . . . And Harry let the "but" dangle in midair with this big, *pregnant*, pause. And finally I made a noise like a drum roll and said, "And the man *was. . . .?*"

And he says, "Out of business." And he laughs this dry little laugh. "He had a *permanent* going out of business sale just before I got there—the really *final* sidewalk clearance sale."

"You mean . . ?"

"Mm-hmm. Killed himself."

"Oh, brother, don't tell me. Uncle Edding. Right?" Sure enough. If Harry didn't have bad luck, he wouldn't've had any luck at all. I remember wondering aloud how it was that somebody with so much money could kill himself.

He flips into his Harry the Younger voice and says, "Einstein? Relativity? To you it's a lot. To him? Me? It was a nice amount. Difference between you'n'me, Daddio. Hey, Jah-gee. It's the reason you live where you do, baby."

I informed him gently that they make six foot long Trojans for people like him: giant pricks. And he flipped back into Harry the Elder—which was really unnerving—and said, "Language, George! Language! Please."

I said something else that got him off on Troy. Oh! I said the way he talked against Fort Edward bothered me. He asked if I remembered my comment about Troy that time he was going to torch that place near Cluett Peabody's. Sure did! My own favorite line: "Whenever I drive through downtown Troy, I want to pull my car over by the Menands bridge, put my head on the steering wheel and have a good cry, it's so depressing." He laughed so hard even I laughed.

"Fort Edward, Mickeyville, all those worn out old river towns? They're just an extension of Troy, George. It's like you said, George, 'And the Lord created the world and he looked for a place to put the enema. And he made Troy.' And Mechanicville and Fort Edward and all the rest of them." He just went right on. Said that was the difference between my generation and his. Mine thinks everything has to stay gloomy, like . . . . How did he say that? Like we're predestined to live the same life we all had in the Depression.

"Heart of My Heart" came on again. I heard him grunt. Boy, he did *not* want to hear that song and I wanted to know why. But he raced right on and said that Edding's business had been in Chicago. Harry ran out of cash very quickly and ended up in a soup line on the Loop. Lived in a mission just off it. I was in Chicago for Midshipman's School in 'forty-two. That was a different time. My time.

Harry had hit bottom. He was penniless. He broomed floors, sported sandwich boards—took anything. Real "Brother Can You Spare a Dime" stuff. He couldn't hear it without getting blue. He actually sang part of it. Beautiful voice. I think that was the first time I felt bad for the guy.

He'd been offered a meal to unload bootleg booze on the South Side. Funny we had that in common in 'thirty-one, helping move bootleg booze. He was in the warehouse where, for whatever reason, they had white phosphorus allotrope—God only knows *why*—and this dumb jamoke was about to pour the water out of the container. Harry screamed at him and got him to stop. I shuddered to think of it. He said, "I mean, George, you took the top award in chemistry. You *know*." And from that moment I began to see that he really knew his stuff. Only later did it occur to me to wonder how he knew about my award at Union. I found out. God, so many steps ahead.

So, the boss calls him into the office and he figures he's dead, because the idiot was Legs Diamond's nephew or some such thing. Instead Gander, that's the head guy, Gander actually slips him a fin. Harry was in heaven. I remember Harry said that Gander thought he spoke funny, because Harry had this upper class accent and that's where he—Harry, I mean—that's where Harry started talking like he's from Brooklyn. I guess Gander wanted to find out how Harry knew about the chemicals and Harry told him how he nearly got his degree in chemical engineering. Of course he had to throw in how he'd been nervous thinking this Grander would resent that he went to Harvard, "like some people resent it." Harry was as subtle as a loud fart in a cathedral.

This Gander asks him if he could mix up a few things and pretty soon he's making explosives. And he says—get this, he makes his voice sound like FDR's—and he says "It was all pretty exotic for a kid who'd sung in the Harvard Glee Club a year before."

I told him I had that very same sensation when I was putting myself through college working at the Watervliet Arsenal. Very exotic. Jesus H. Christ. I put myself through school and the only goddamn person who ever helped me was Jane. My own mother made me pay room and board and all her cheap brother George ever gave me was carfare. I was named for him and all the cheap bastard could give me was carfare? He was a doctor, for God sakes. He had more money than God. I wish I'd—Holy Mary help me stop this coughing!—*I* wish I'd never been named for you, you cheap bastard. A doctor with no kids and all you can. . . Jesus, Jesus, I can't take this pain. I need to live a little longer. Okay?

All right, all right, I'm back. I had to take some time out. My God, this is hard. It's exhausting. I'm having a hard time remembering here. We were getting near Saratoga? In Saratoga? I was distracted trying to figure out how to get to Piping Rock unnoticed. He was going on about, oh, I don't know, something about blowing things up for this guy. Learned a lot from working with vets who'd been in munitions, lot of really skilled men no one wanted after the Crash. I remember asking him if he thought about going back to Harvard on the GI Bill. All he said was, "I'm going to buy Harvard someday." His elevator had definitely stopped on eight—Section 8.

Somehow he got off on onto how he launched his career after that. He had to blow up this huge wooden warehouse on the docks. He told Gander it'd be better to make it look natural. So, he cellophaned the key points of the building and torched it. Instant success! Suddenly he's in demand to torch these huge old mansions for families who needed the insurance. He boo-hooed about torching a Stanford White house. I didn't say that Jennie and I stayed in one when I was stationed in Newport in forty-three. Well, he says, better that than ending up as a boarding house or a Union Avenue dorm for rich little Skiddies. He called them "*grande dames.*" The mansions, I mean. Said they're gentility and shouldn't be treated so shabbily.

He's waving his good arm and saying how he'll probably have to put the rest of those poor old "*grande dames*" on Union out of their misery some day. Phew. Made me shudder. I tried to say that if he wanted to talk about shabby treatment, he should see the way some of those Skiddies treated my mother. She was a Skidmore housemother. But he was obsessed. "People nowadays, George, they're so used to *nothing*. *Nothing!* Live in little ticky-tacky Levitttown crap. No quality like in the twenties. Or, worse, living in trailers!" Oh, God, yes. How could I *ever* forget *that*? He went on and on and *on* about trailers and about the country going down the toilet. But *he* was "doing something about it." That's what he said. Yes, dear friends, Mr. Cuckoo was taking care of it.

Mr. Cuckoo was on that and all the while I'm driving along wondering how I could be chauffeuring an arsonist to help burn down the Piping Rock. And somebody so insane? Well, anyway, we'd started to roll into Saratoga and my heart's thumping and I'm saying to him that I prefer not to ride down Broadway. I started to turn off before Van Raalte's to go over Nelson. Harry says keep heading for Broadway. *Why*? Get this: he wants to go to Willy Lum's for Chinese. *Holy Christ!* I threw a seven, "You want chink food? *Now*? Are you absolutely nuts? Go to Willy Lum's right now? " I kept shouting "Right now?" at him. I remember him trying to shush me, like a baby, and I screamed at him, "Shit! Let's just hit the Colonial for a round? Huh? Have one with Frank Sullivan and Monty Woolley? Maybe visit Diamond Jim Brady'n'Lillian Russ . . . ."

Oh, Christ, my chest! Oh, Christ, oh, Christ . . . . You know what was amaz . . . ? Oh, Christ, Oh, shit! Sorry. It's hard to control. [*There is a long silence.*]

Anyways—and this is amazing—he says, very calmly, like a kid talking about a movie star, "Do you think we could see them?"

"Diamond Jim and Lillian are dead, Harry."

And he gets condescending and whines at me, "No, Georgie. I mean Sullivan. Woolley. Come onnnn . . . . This is a side'a'you I never saw."

The boy was *really* scaring me. Oh, do not buy any cashews, Mother, we have enough nuts at home. "Sure thing. We'll burn down Piping Rock, then stop by Frank's to say hello." He sighed this big sigh. Like this.

Sorry, I forget that makes me cough so. Anyway, I understood his point. I took for granted that Frank lived just up Lincoln from us. He was so nice to us, to Jane. Of course I saw him and Woolley a lot. Woolley was always in the store or at Frank's. I mean—and this is the truth—the night my daughter was born? Frank and Monty picked me up at the hospital in a cab and took me over to the Colonial for a 'toddy,' as Frank called it. God! They got me *stinking* drunk, took me home in a cab, tucked me into bed and *then* went *back* out to finish the night. I thought I could drink, but those boys? They were sports!

I wanted to die like a sport. Now look at me—can't even go out that way. Unh, unh. Oh, God, my arm! I'm going to check out with a heart cond . . . unh, unh, let me go fast? Got to . . . Oh, God, I don't want to go this goddamn minute! Got to . . . concentrate. Okay, okay. Okay. So, I see Harry's staying on this kick. He's not going to stop about seeing them. We were close to Van Raalte's. I pulled over by the Old Red Spring, got out and left the car running, left him in the car jabbering like a magpie. I cupped my hands and slurped the water. He came over and did the same. I was happy for a moment's peace. I said, "So, let's just shoot over Nelson and forget all this." No! We have to drive down Broadway.

And then I'm yelling at him: "*I CAN'T*!" People know me here! Hundreds. Cops. Frank. My neighbors. My mother. My own *mother* still lives on Spring Street! My kid's godfather's right on Broadway. Ned Rowland? The Arcade liquor store?"

Sorry. God, my chest. Sorry. I've got to stop yelling. I have *got* to get this done. Come on, George. Come on, boy. Concentrate!

He gave me a lot of crap about Ned's family being part of Saratoga's Mick Mafia. We got in the car and I tried to go a back way toward the casino, but Mr. Crackpot is back on going to Willy Lum's and then he said, "You don't have a choice, George. But, trust me. I know why we need to go there." I don't know why, but out of the blue I said—*very* calmly—"Joe Adonis tell you to? Meyer Lansky, maybe?" And I hit the gas and we took off.

And I'll tell you this for free, it's *truly* amazing when you can actually *feel* something you've said has struck a nerve, especially in a dark car, with the radio playing, the tires slowly kah-thumping on the concrete, and the other person not saying a word. Amazing when you just know it. I knew. I always thought the worst torture for a man would be to hang him by thumbs under the hot noon sun, stark naked, and once an hour come out and rap him soundly on the testicles with a soup spoon. The waiting would be as bad as the pain. So I decided to wait. In fact, I was going to change the topic, but the radio did it for me.

The reception was incredible after nightfall. He had on classical music out of New York and I was beginning to long for bebop. I hit a big bump and it shifted the tuning a bit—and what comes on? "Heart of My Heart"!

Well, he made a dive, but I was too quick and slammed my hand over it and barked, "Leave it!" I think he was quite startled, because he sat back. I couldn't take it any more. I was so tense and —I have to admit this, though God forgive me I'm ashamed to, I was a bit excited. I was smoking like a chimney and jumpy and sick of his bullshit and I said, "What the hell's with that song? And don't give me any *crap* about a woman."

He says, "My godfather was a Latin scholar." I told him that he'd had me wondering before, but now *that* explained everything. He just ignored me and said, "*Cor cordis mei.*"

"WHAT?"

He said it again. "'*Cor cordis mei.*' It's what my godfather inscribed in a book of Latin proverbs he gave me the year before I graduated from prep school. '*Cor cordis mei.*' Heart of My Heart." The godfather loved him as a son. "The Gang That Sang Heart of My Heart," was popular in 'twenty-six. Harry still had that book in Chicago when he owned nothing else in the world. He was standing on a soup line and heard a guy in back of him say he had taught Latin at Northwestern. "Imagine. A Latin scholar begging a bowl of soup." He looked at the man and then at that book. It was the last thing he had left from his old life, outside of his parents—and inside it is the name of the man who destroyed them. He gave the book to the Latin scholar who was so surprised. Harry says, "And I was so relieved. I've hated that song ever since."

All right, song puzzle solved. Why are we going to Willy Lum's? It was part of it, he said. We have to go there. "Just go?" he asks me. "And stop asking so many questions?" He'll tuck a few bob extra in the kit for me, he says. "Trust me."

"And you'll respect me in the morning." I took a deep breath. "What the hell. Why not? Tell you what, Harry, let's roll down Broadway, stick our heads out the windows, whistle at the cops and tell'em what great legs they have." Harry actually laughed. He made this pansy voice and said, "Oh, yoo-hoo. Mith-ter poe-LEETH man. Oh, yoo-hoo." He cracked me up. He was good. Sounded like a real fruit.

We came to Steigerwald's gas station and I pulled out onto Broadway. Harry went quiet. By the time we got down by City Hall and the police station, my heart was *pounding* in my ears. I was *sweating* gallons. God, I am right now. God, I'm *drenched* thinking of it. I can hear him saying, again and again, "Not to worry." Set of balls, I'll say that.

There were a lot of cars, people in my old watering holes. It was the season. Suddenly Harry starts waving his arms like he owns Broadway. It's all different, he says. Not the same Saratoga since they closed the clubs in 'fifty. He was right. It was different, I was thinking. And it was going to be a *helluva lot* different after tonight.

We were coming up on that part of Broadway by MacFinn's and just at that moment, some idiot stalled his car and cars bunched up in back of us. We can't move. I was gripping the wheel hard. He knew I was shaking, and he was talking a mile a minute to distract me. We ran through the periodic table. Talked about the number of different kinds of alcohol. I had to correct him. It was one hundred thirty-seven, not thirty-eight.

We were stopped dead for a few minutes right across from MacFinn's. "Miss it?" he said. I told him I didn't miss the season, the long hours and the touts, the phonies and the goddamn pushy New Yorkers. I looked over at him and apologized. No offense. He's a Long Islander, not some New Yorker like his mother's big-mouthed cousin from Brooklyn. "So," I thought, "there's the accent."

"Hey, Georgie! You remember Picker Van Dyne, the tout? He's goin' around town telling everybody *he's* the model for Nicely Nicely in *Guys and Dolls*." Everyone thought Picker got his name from picking up tickets. It was from picking his shorts out of his crack all the time. Harry gagged. "Picker's a walking rectum" I said. "I dealt with so many of 'em in MacFinn's, I could've been a proctologist." That got him laughing. Got us both laughing. I needed laughing. I needed him laughing.

I looked at MacFinn's. Was it two years or two minutes since I'd left in August of 'fifty-two? Now it's August of 'fifty-four and I'm driving a guy who was a ghost for a lot of people.

"Nice people there?" he asks me, still distracting me. I needed that. Yes. A lot of really nice people. Chili and Ethel—the girls on the soda fountain—they had class. Never gawked at the famous people who were customers. We had a lot of 'em. "Phillip Morris Johnny used to come into the store'n do his famous call—'Call for Phil-lip *Mah*-ris!'" I imitated his "Call for Phil-lip *Mah*-ris!" a few times. Harry laughed so hard. Johnny was so small. Once my son Mike stood by him and said he liked Johnny because he was the only grown-up his size. I think Mike was, what? Seven at the time?

Yeah, well. What was I saying? Stalled car . . . oh! Did I say that? The driver's drunk and now cops are directing us around him. I'm *shaking*. Harry's still trying to talk me down. "Talk about the famous people in Saratoga, George." The Williams Brothers summering by us on Lincoln Avenue—before Andy went solo. Sophie Tucker came in MacFinn's. Jennie and I'd saw her at Piping Rock. And Joe E. Lewis. People you had to go to New York to see.

"You go to New York a lot, George?" Jennie and I did—stayed at the Warwick. Manager was summer customer. I'd treat him right. He'd treat us right. Got us in all the clubs—Nick's in the Village, La Vie en Rose uptown. At this point, I was **FINALLY** pulling out and around the car and Harry's asking, in his *important* voice, if I knew that Monte Proser ran La Vie en Rose. "Sure," I said, "Booked all the Piping Rock acts. Customer of mine. Sure I know who Proser is."

"Hey, hey, Georgie! You stay at Lansky's favorite hotel and you know Proser? Wow, dad!" I should've listened when he said that but I was hearing Junior and I didn't want Junior. He just ran right on, "Hey Georgie! Know where the Piping Rock name is from?"

I didn't. He says, "The Island. Locust Valley. Know it?"

It didn't matter. I was supposed to. If he did, then the world did. "Locust Valley's not that far from where I live," he said.

We're moving slowly. My blood was already pounding in my ears and I was concentrating on my knuckles. "You *live*?" I said. He says he has a place—near the old family pile, which, some day, he's going to buy it back. My God, the man's a cuckoo clock. He on about how "Fawther" was a member in all the same clubs with *them* on the North Shore—sailing, polo. He flipped the Zippo once and said, in this deadly calm voice, "They all played with him. And then they all toyed with him. Then they cut him out and hurt him. I shall hurt them." It makes your skin crawl when a man talks that calmly about hurting people and you know he can and you're sure he will.

We finally inched past MacFinn's. I was joking to shake off my nerves'n'said, "Should stop at MacFinn's, pick up a Brownie. Take some snaps of the Great Event." And get this? Harry thanks me and says no, he's covered all that. I understood when we got to the club.

I pulled down Caroline and onto Putnam. Broadway's quite a bit more elevated than Putnam. You drop a story anyway and you can see the exposed basement walls of those Broadway buildings. We pulled up near the back of Willy Lum's, close to the Hathorn Spring. Willy Lum's had been a legit theater once and the back still had the high fly gallery. He says, "Chow mein? Lo mein?" I'd gotten all the oriental chink food I'd ever wanted in the South Pacific. No thank you. I still drink green tea, though. Habit I picked up in the Navy, like having my Filipino cabin boy. Lost that benefit when I couldn't reenlist.

It seemed like an hour until he came out with an eggroll and a big brown paper bag. I jumped when he climbed in and said, "It's safe to go."

"Safe to go?" I wondered. Who the hell gave him the go-ahead?

He shoves a thermos at me. "Stow this, mister. Manhattans. Steady the nerves. Figured you'd need a few," he says. I might've, but I wouldn't say that to him. He kept shoving the thermos at me, saying, "Have one," and I kept asking him, "How come?" until he answered, "Because now I'm going to tell you why we're torching the Piping Rock."

I know I just sat there with my mouth just hanging open like a cow. Just when you think you have figured it all out.

CHAPTER 12

Hold on a minute. I don't know what's going on. Hold on . . . . St-stay put.

Brother. Let me get a drink. [*He sings going out and coming back.*] "And the music goes round and round, oh, oh, oh, oh, oh-oh, and it comes out . . . ." Augh, oh! This is unbeliev . . . my tablets? Where're they? *Where? Where?* Okay, okay. There . . . .

All right. I'm avoiding this. Listen. Listen. There's a point—you know what it is—there's a point where, if you're an adult and you've lived, you know. That point where the truth is evident? Might not be a hundred percent evident, but the truth is there and you know when you're only being told a fraction of it.

Yes. It's . . . it's like, like a point on the horizon. It's that point on the horizon. It's moving toward you, but you don't acknowledge the truth of it. Then, slowly, you do. You're standing there, taking a leak off the stern. The point grows larger, getting closer and your sense . . . of . . . what? Your, your sense of survival is *screaming* at you: "*Acknowledge what you see.*" *Acknowledge* what you see as *being* there. And, and some stupid sense of *having* to finish pissing is *overwhelming* your common sense. You know? You feel . . . God . . . you feel, you can't just *run* and *urinate* on yourself. You have your legs braced and your wake is *huge* and you're so tired you can't even believe you're standing. It's all in seconds and it grows bigger and then you see wings and then you *know*. And you know that you know. It's a Zero. And then you're shaking that thing and buttoning up and you're screaming, "*Stations! Stations! Get to stations.*" I'm screaming, "Get to stations! **Get to your stations**!" My boys are scrambling. I see Hilly and the others and they are screaming and taking their stations and throwing everything at that Jap as he comes in and banks and strafes the deck. His guns rip right through the bottom of that thick metal plate shielding on our fifty and, just, just, Christ! Just **RIP** it right off. **Slice** it right off, so it flies like a saucer. "Down! Down! Down! Down! Down! Down! Down! *Hit the deck!* Hit the deck! Hit the deck! Jesus! *Down! Get down, get down!*"

But it's too late. Too late. It decapitates him. Slices his head right off. [*Gasping.*] Oh, oh, oh, oh, oh . . . I can't st . . . stop crying. Oh, oh, oh, oh, oh . . . I'm, I'm looking right at him and there's no head. He's still firing. Still firing! Then he rolls off the side of the seat, 'cause he's not even strapped in. Oh-oh-oh-oh. . . Blood's everywhere. I'm hit in the legs. Blood coming through my pants and I look over and see Ross. I'm still moving. Oh, Jesus, no, please, not another man. I know he's good as dead. He's looking up at me and his lips are moving, but, there's blood in his mouth, and, and I know he's good as dead. I kneel down and I'm holding him. "Hail Mary, full of grace . . ." I'm crying and he's just blank. "Hail Mary, full of grace. Say it with me, Ross. Say it, Rossie. Hang on, Rossie. Hang on. No, you can't hang on, can you, can you? Aw. Ross. You're gone. You're dead." He is. He's dead. He's dead. [*Long silence*]

Aw, Jesus, I'm sorry. What's the matter with me? I'm like those old vets in Joyce's, crying in their beers. Oh-oh-oh-oh. Oh, my God, it was awful. Oh-oh-oh-oh. Why, why, why?

Sorry. I just had to walk away for a few minutes. Anyways, okay . . . anyways, let's get . . . back to the point. This point where you know? I knew when he said he was going to tell me why we were burning the Piping Rock that he wasn't going to tell me, even though he said he was. At best I'd get *part* of the truth, because all he ever did was lie and tell people parts of the truth. And how much of what his truth was? I, I didn't know. But I was going to find out, because I felt . . . . Felt? **FELT**? Christ, I *knew, I knew* my life depended upon it.

I didn't press him. No. I'd take my time. I drove up Phila, toward the flat track, saying I wanted to avoid Spring Street House, because it's where Annie lived. Harry gave me this, uh, this ah, perplexed, mm, annoyed, "*Huh?*" The jackass. I reminded him that about her being a house mother at Skidmore. I said I had this vision of her out there at midnight, red goddamn hair waving in the breeze, spotting me as I drove by. She'd be out there with her fourteen-gallon mop pail mopping the steps. My stepfather always said she cleaned so much he was going to have a fourteen-gallon mop pail carved on her stone. And then she outlived him. Two marriages. Twice widowed. Harry laughed at that. I wanted him to laugh. He's not telling me anything. I needed him to laugh.

We swung back over to Union. It's a big, wide street. It was filled with cars. It was late, but cars were still out. Harry was slouched down in the seat with his knees up on the dash. He had these sharp cheekbones and really looked like a kid. I'm young looking, you know? Well, I mean I was. Even at fifty I was taken for forty. But this guy? My Lord . . . . My Lord. I remember him saying something about how it was hard to understand what everyone did for fun now that the clubs and Lake Houses were all closed. I had to agree with that. With the big bands gone and Riley's and Newman's and the Piping Rock gone. . . . He. . . .

I can't do this. I . . . I can't do this! **For Christ sakes, I can't do this! Christ Jesus!** I *can't!* God, God, oh Father, I am sorry but I *can't!* Why'd I ever think I could? I can't *talk* about this anymore! I can't go *on* with this! I can't! I just *can't!* Where's the switch to this goddamn thing?

[*It must have been that same night, not much later. The recorder comes on, but he says nothing at first. There's the sound of footsteps moving back and forth, a sign for those of us who knew him that he was fretting.*]

All right. All *right*. Let's get this monkey off my back. Let's be a man about this, eh George? No sense starting and not finishing. Whoever hears this? I, I swear this is true. And I swear I never. . .unh, unh, oh God . . . I swear, I swear I never meant for it to happen this way.

So, we . . . catch my breath . . . we, so we, we were up on Union. I remember I said I'd like one of those mansions and he corrected me and said, "'Big house' George. Not 'mansion.' We call them 'big houses.'" If you're poor the big house is a jail. Rich and it's a mansion.

Did he live in a "big house" before his godfather? Not exactly, he said. Definitely not like his godfather. "'Fawtha," he says, "had no such pretensions." No, I told, him. Fawtha was just a simple country boy. I laughed so hard, I coughed in my trousers! He ignored me. No, their house was rather—sorry, rawtha—their house was rawtha like these on Union. A "smidgeon smaller" he said. Jane always used smidgeon. He moaned on about how sad it was so many of these *grandes dames* were dorms or, worse, boarding houses for touts and cheapies. Over and over he kept saying, "I'm going to hate to have to do it."

I wanted to shut him up, but I had to schmooze him, tell me what was really happening. Had he been hired? No. Not yet, he says. He'd done the Mabee house in `thirty-seven, but that was as a personal favor. Jesus, I'd never even heard of it, but he went on about that for five minutes. But when he finally got started here, he said, he'd be clearing away a big problem for the generations to come. His words, trust me. "Times will be better and they'll want their own architecture," he says. So, Mr. Arson will come with his special Studebaker and clean the slate. The boy left his rudder in drydock when they slipped him out of the berth.

All of a sudden he bellows, "Hey, slow down. We're early." *Early?* What's all this? We meeting somebody there, I ask him? Lord, God, my heart was *racing*. He's cool as a cucumber. Says he's made arrangements to ensure *nobody* is there. He and the others have this thing timed down to a science. Others, always "the others."

I swung a hard right onto Nelson and headed for Lincoln. And get this. He's fiddling with the fucking radio trying to get something called Tex and Jinx, whatever the hell that was, but I didn't say anything to Mr. Hah-vahd for fear I'd get a frigging lecture on that. "Siro's?" I ask him. No, not Siro's. Could be recognized by people he grew up with. Witnesses are fine, but not anybody who really knows him. I didn't get it. "Who'd recognize you, Harry? It's what, twenty-something years? You look different, right?" He said I wouldn't understand. But I did later.

He's driving me nuts flipping the dial. I swing down Lincoln. Suddenly he sighs like he's in ecstasy and says, "Ah! WOR." And thankfully big band music comes out. I needed something to settle me. What I really needed was a drink. The street was jammed with cars. Big Lincolns and Caddies.

We came up on Frank Sullivan's house. It was all dark. Sure. Frank was out drinking and Kate was long asleep. He asks what's cooking and I point Frank's house out to him. He acts like we were passing Christ's house. Makes me pull up in front and pours me a Manhattan. Ahhhhh. I was in love! He says, just one. He's nervous about idling here too long. I say, "Relax, don't get your hemorrhoids in an uproar. All the cops know me. I'll say I'm down visiting Frank."

"Geeze," he says, like a starstruck teen. A ball of contradictions is Harry the Younger. It was, shall we say, strange sitting in a car on my old street drinking Manhattans out of a thermos—but I took the first one on an inhale. It helped. I was, shall we say, able to sit up and take further nourishment.

I'm halfway into Manhattan number two and Harry the Elder pipes up, "Frank Sullivan was right."

"Sure, Harry. Anything you say."

"No. What Frank wrote in the *Times* about Joe McCarthy.' I'm blank. "Kefauver hearings?" He's *very* sarcastic. "Read more than the *Daily News* and you would." I told him to use a razorblade for a suppository.

He takes this fatherly tone, like he's speaking to the village idiot: "Sullivan said Joe McCarthy would want to use TV the way Kefauver did. So, Sullivan was right, all right? He was right, all right" and, natch, repeats "he was right, all right?" a hundred times. He started bitching about

McCarthy—and then MacArthur again. I told him "Don't start that crap again." He said that the real reason MacArthur had Eisenhower beat his father was because "Fawtha" had his tent pitched right next to a Negro man. When he said "Negro man" he just spit it out and I thought he was disgusted with dear old dad, but no! Turns out this *Negro* man had fought right in the trenches with his father. Side by side! That was strange to me. We never mixed with Negroes in the service, except for porters or cabin boys. I had a Filipino cabin boy. My little brown brother took good care of me, he did. Coffee on time and shirts done perfectly. Missed that when I got back. But we never had *Negroes* fighting along with us.

So, Harry's on and on about injustice and all that. A starry-eyed dreamer, like my kids. Why . . . my arm, unh, unh . . . why couldn't . . . my kids . . .? Shit! Why couldn't they ever do anything normal? What'd we fight for in the war? What'd we work for? What'd we work for, Jennie? This is it? *This* is it? Christ! And I'm going to die like th . . . unh. . . . . oh, my . . . oh, my God, my chest is killing me! Maybe Harry was right. Maybe the end of the War was the end of the world. I mean, what happened after? What *happened*? Everything I hoped f. . . unh! . . . gone . . . . everything I want for my kids they don't want? Joe goes to Fordham—*Fordham*! Not Notre Dame, like I wanted, but Fordham's good. I thought he'd be a lawyer, be rich. I told him—I told him, I said, "I can't understand you. Why don't you want that? I'd want that if I were you." He says I just didn't understand. What's to understand? You become a lawyer, you get rich and you do what you want. I said this to Jane one night and she says—*get this*—she says, "At least he's happy." At least he's happy! At least he's *happy*! *Christ*! "Happy? *Happy*?" I yell at her, "Jesus *Christ*, Jane! There are more important things in life than being happy!" She just laughed at me.

[*There is a long silence.*] Enough of this shit. Let me get a beer. Jesus, I can't waste my energy on. . . unh. . .on. . . I mean, this is hard to talk about. Come on, George. Come on. *Come on.* We were sitting in front of Frank's. I was really ripping into the Manhattans. Harry seemed to have a gallon. Crazy son of a bitch! I did *not* want to be there, sitting so near to our house. I remember looking up at Frank's house and suddenly I wanted to go in and beg him to make this all stop. Which if you think about it, that was crazy. What could Frank do?

Harry lit a cigarette. I thought about how he loved that flame and about how *old* his eyes were. I looked at the windshield. "This is insane, Harry."

And he agreed. He *agreed*! I mean, I thought he did. Then he gives this insane answer. He says. . .he says, "You're absolutely right, George. The world slid into insanity in the Depression and hasn't come out of it since."

I remember those words like missal Latin. "The world slid into insanity in the Depression and hasn't come out of it since." The world wasn't the only thing that had slid into madness. Then he—oh God, I hated him for this—then he said something that, that just made me sadder than I think I've ever been. "Our world ended after the war, George." I couldn't speak for anyone else, but I knew mine had. God, I know mine had.

I couldn't . . I didn't want . . . what am I trying to say here? It was like I was trapped on memory lane and I couldn't get out. I slipped it in gear we passed slowly by Chuck and Anne Maddox' house. I double-parked. You lived here, he says? No, two doors down. This is Chuck Maddox' house, I say. Chuck was with Patton's Third. Never the same after that. Never.

Harry said the whole truth when he said, "None of us ever were."

I pointed up at a second floor window and said that one afternoon, a few years before, Chuck'd had an argument with our neighbor. Just pure luck that I saw Chuck's B.A.R., pointing out the window at the guy. I went upstairs and, casually, you know, very casually, I said, 'What's up, Chuck?' He didn't look up but said, in a very calm voice, 'I'm going to kill him, George.'"

Harry said, "I understand that."

I talked him out of it. Now he's dead. This year he shot himself.

"Mm-hmm. I understand that."

I knew he did. I did. We sat there forever—probably just a few minutes—windows down, both of us smoking, not talking. I'd gotten tired of Harry's bumming cigarettes, so I had tossed him his own pack. "Let's get going," I said. "Get it over with?" He pointed to our old house. Did I miss it? I told him I didn't want to talk about it I just want to get this done. It was okay if he wanted to blab about his life. I'm not this big sentimentalist. Just not one to dwell on the past and I sure as hell didn't want to look back on that part of my life. If I'd never run to get out of Saratoga, I never would've ended up at the Piping Rock. Jesus, Jennie, you were right. I should have stayed with E. R. Squibb. Should've stayed in sales. Never should've gone to work in Saratoga. *Never.* Oh, God, just tell me. Why did you ever let me do that? Why did everything have to get so crazy? Why did you have to let everything get so crazy?

Oh, Jesus. [*Long silence.*]

I'd give a tender portion of my anatomy for a cigarette. All right, so I realized he was trying to push Manhattans on me. Maybe he thought it'd make me a little mellower, but I get mean on booze and I was getting mean then. I wasn't liking this trip down memory lane and the booze wasn't helping. I asked him if he were trying to slip me a mickey. Ooo, gracious! He, shall we say, got a little touchy? Hah!

I can't remember what happened then, but we ended up back on Union. I'm mean now. I remember that. I'm saying, isn't it time we get out of Saratoga? Forget the whole thing? And he's telling me to slow down and he starts yelling, "Pull over! PULL *OVER!*" He's groping under his knees. I hear a clicking noise and know he's slid out another drawer and think to myself, "Oh, shit, he's got another gun. This is it," and, idiot that I am, I'm thinking that I'd just pull over, just run as fast as I can, but before I can do that he has this wad that he jams his hand at my face.

"*Here!*" he's screaming at me, "Here! Take it! Take it, you fucker!" I put my hand up real quick to protect myself, although, I mean—Lord!—if he's gonna shoot me, what the hell good was my hand? And then, *wham!* He hits me right in the temple with a wad of money. "Two gees!" he's screaming, "two gees! Take it, take it!" The grand promised and another "g" to get me to shut up. He says, "You're going. We're torching the Piping Rock and you're shutting your fucking mouth or somehow I'll torch it alone and our two girlfriends will be my insurance that *you* go to bed every night in Comstock, getting it up the old dirt road by a guy named Louie."

I was shaking, but I put that two grand up to my lips and said to him, "Just as long as I get a kiss."

CHAPTER 13

He called me some sweet nothings. Terrible thing when a man lacks a sense of humor. The blackmailing bastard shoved that stupid hat down on his eyebrows and jammed his knees up on the dash like a kid and grumbled like one. It wouldn't have bothered me except that now he was really starting to, um . . . . Well . . . how do I say this? He was going in and out of being Harry the Younger. It was horribly uncomfortable and I knew at this rate he wasn't going to tell me why we were really going to torch the Piping Rock. I needed Harry the Elder back—but how to do that? Then it came to me! I asked him how it was he came to burn down his godfather's house.

Oh, heavenly day! I scored a double on that one! He acts like he's savoring those Cuban cigars we used to sell and, honestly, I know he didn't even realized he said it happened a year after he met Joe Adonis. [*The tape is damaged here. A few sentences are fragmented.*] Okay, so Joe's . . . [*kn*]own him eighteen years . . . . Bingo, I . . . thought . . . the word puzzles . . . the mind sharp . . . come out in early . . . ber. Mr. Adonis'd hear . . . liked . . . he calls him "Mr. Adonis". . . fear'n'a little respect there. . . in Brooklyn, did some jobs here and there . . . Adonis and was doing. . .big hurricane of thirty-eight hit . . . I remem . . .? September twenty-first, exact date . . . at a Lowe's watching a newsreel a day'er'two days later with this dolly.

"Your wife?" I ask. Not his wife. His wife'd left him. She wanted to be Stella Dallas. Problem was, she had the society boy without the money. Harry was chain-smoking a mile a minute—even to me and I smoked four packs a day. He kept tapping the one end of the Luckies pack on the dash. It kept getting a little faster and a little faster and a little faster as he talked and he starts bobbing around like Harry the Younger. I know I've said it, but this boy was driving a train with *no* tracks.

So, anyways, he's playing grab-ass in the cheap seats and the newsreel announcer starts on about the hurricane and, wham! There's his godfather on the *screen*! Harry stops stone still and, get this, his blonde bombshell booms out in this Betty Boop voice—and he *made* his voice sound just like Betty Boop's— "'Whatsamattah? Ain't my titties good enough faw-yuz?'" I mean, *just* like Betty Boop. Hah, hah, hah! He could be funny when he wasn't being insane.

Sorry . . . got stop . . . aw-unh . . .sorry. I'm really coughing up something here.

Sorry. I'm back. So, Uncle Ned's doing the washboard weeper routine about the storm wiping out his beach house and he's uninsured and boo-hoo-hoo. Harry slips the blonde fifty, tells her to take a powder, and drives to Garden City like a madman. Luck of the would-be Irish, not only is nobody home, but that end of town has a power outage. Harry went through the house with a fine . . . .

Oh, Jesus, oh, Jesus . . . my chest . . . .

[*It is quiet for some time.*] Sorry. Anyways, Uncle Ned had sold of a lot of things. Probably couldn't make it on his own without Harry's father to milk. *But!* The imbecile had all the company books hidden away, *plus* a record of all his deals and how he cooked the books. Can you believe that? Keeping records like some Nazi? Maybe he was t. . . . Unh! Oh, *God.* Hang on a sec. Oh, God! Unh, unh. Oh, my *God!* Oh, I think, I think. . . unh, unh. I think I. . .

Sorry. Didn't mean to puke on you. . . . Why the hell am I *sorry?* I'm dying. If you hear this, this is what it's like. It's symptomatic. Who will hear this?

Where was I? Aside from gently tossing my cookies down the front of my skivvies? Let's see. I said he burned down the house? No. Um . . . Okay, Harry jury-rigged enough lighting to work and taped the house. He had balls, that boy. Never worried about the neighbors. "If you act like you belong, people assume you belong." S'what he said.

He was telling me all this and flipping that damn Zippo open and shut and open and shut, and then he lit the Zippo and the flame jumped about four inches from his eyes. Oh, those eyes. Brrrr . . . . He laughed as he said he burned down that house that Ned had stolen. I was scared. I was *scared.* But I have to admit he added a touch of class to it. He called Ned and whispered in the receiver, "Ned? Harry here. '*Cor cordis mei.*' I burned your house down." How he laughed!

You know, I wrote down a lot of this later for safekeeping, but what Ned said I could not have forgotten if I'd tried. Ned doesn't call Harry a bastard—these are Harvard folks, remember. Instead Ned says, "*Nulla avarita sine poena est.*" And, God knows where it came from, but without batting an eyelash I said to Harry, "Seneca. 'No avarice without penalty.'" High school Latin. Harry didn't say anything, but I knew he was impressed.

Harry told Ned he was going to torch everything Ned owned, one at a time—not including the Locust Valley house, but he didn't tell Ned that.

Ned threatened to call the cops and Harry told him about the books. Harry laughed as he said that. It was eerie coming out of the dark. Harry had that Zippo going and he'd flipped the Zippo cover—click!—as he said how he'd burn them down, Ned would rebuild them, and he'd burn them down again. Harry clicked the Zippo cover each time he'd say it: "He'd rebuild'em." Click! "I'd burn'em down." Over and over. "Rebuild'em," click, "burn'em," click. "Rebuild'em," click, "burn'em," click.

Now we were heading out for the Piping Rock and my heart was pounding and I was lightheaded. My lower back hurt and I was afraid it'd spasm. From the war? Awful when it went. It wasn't helping that the closer we got to the casino the more he became Harry the Younger. I felt as nervous as I did during the Philippine Invasion. Harry? Harry's cool as a cuke, discussing how he earned his Eagle Scout in arson.

So, Harry sighs deeply and says how "wonderful" it got. "Now it's nineteen forty-one. Ned's had had a couple of big heart attacks and he'd disappeared. I found him here in Saratoga, Georgie." Ned was at the Gideon Putnam . . . hotel for newly-weds and nearly-deads. Ned's going to the Lincoln Baths, trying for a cure with exercise and mineral baths— Schott's method I'd say—and meanwhile trying to tap a few Locust Valley cronies.

"Ned was stupid, Georgie. He ratted me out to one of his friends who helped Ned screw dad." That was the only time Harry'd called him anything but Fawtha. "I torched his friend's garage and telephoned Ned, and said, 'Adsum,' which means, 'I am here.' And Ned says to me, 'Tell me you didn't burn Dickie's garage.'" He was begging.

Harry flipped the Zippo. "I told him I did. He screamed at me that I was crazy. '*Amantes sunt amentes*, Ned,' I said to him, which means . . . ."

"'*Lovers are lunatics*,'" I said.

"Reet, Jahgie. You're good, Dad! Ned killed himself in the Lincoln Baths. I'll always love Saratoga for that."

I tried to keep my voice steady. "You're just a sentimentalist Harry."

"Poetic justice for Fawtha."

Did I say Fawtha shot himself in 'thirty-seven? Yep, he did. I never found out what happened to the mother.

Small Manhattan won't hurt. Okay. Back. Mmmmm, that's good. Okay, let's see. Where was I? Umm . . . oh, sure. Ned left a suicide note. Natch. Harry's responsible. Natch. Ned's son calls Harry. Natch. Harry, the Boy

Wonder, meets the son in a Garden City diner, tells him everything and—
get this—shoves the books in sonny boy's face. Sonny recognizes the
handwriting and sees it on the wall at the same time. Harry packs up the
books, pays for breakfast, and leaves Sonny sobbing in his Wheaties.

I didn't know what to say, so I said, "Nice touch buying the kid
breakfast."

"Well, Pyrrhic victory. I mean Ned's friends went after me. That's how
I got arrested in Oyster Bay. Of course, noblesse oblige, I got the choice of
service or jail. Hell, they ran the draft board."

He was quiet for a few moments, just flicking his Zippo open and shut.
Then he said, "Shall we get on with the roast?"

It was so insane, boys and girls, so insane. He was so insane. I was so
scared.

CHAPTER 14

We drove out Union Avenue without a word, smoking like chimneys, rolling past the *big houses* like a slow motion movie. For all the talk, I hadn't heard why we were heading to torch the Piping Rock. I was a nervous wreck.

Across from the track entrance I saw those two bars that sit side by side, "Mike and Joe's" and "King's." My boys, Mike and Joe, thought they were named for them. Kids. The track was closed and quiet. You could see lights on here and there, a small speck of a cigarette glowing in the dark by the Oklahoma. We cruised out past the Yaddo entrance. Jennie loved the Yaddo. It was all crickets and starlight in those days. Union just went right on out, no Northway or anything; pretty quiet and countryside with some mansions, I mean big houses, casinos and ex-casinos.

We were almost there. My *God*, I was scared. Then, bang! There it was, the Piping Rock, all dark, dead. Seemed to get even emptier as we drove up to it. So different from before. As my headlights hit it, you could see it was beginning to look—what? Not overgrown. Unused, I guess. I just wanted to get this done. I cut the lights as we rolled in—I didn't want to attract anyone's attention at the Meadowbrook, which was on the other side of Gilbert. I stopped to let him out. He headed for the back on foot and I started to back the car in to hide it. Thankfully the moon was down by the time we got there.

Suddenly, he's back like a pistol shot, slamming his hand on the car roof, jumping in the front seat and shouting, "Hit it! Hit it! Hit it! Punch that baby!" He didn't have to draw *me* a map! I punched the gas and we were Seabiscuit out of the gate.

"What's up?"

"Drive, just drive!" he's screaming, looking over his shoulder all the time. I'd left the lights off and we were up to seventy, seventy-five in seconds. He starts giving orders and I told him to can it. I knew where we had to go. We went out Union Avenue toward Saratoga Lake. I know there were lights in back of us, but I couldn't tell if they'd followed us out. I took a right turn on two wheels and took us along Lake Lonely. And that place isn't named Lake Lonely for nothing. Brrrrr . . . . I left the lights off for a while, figuring we'd take our chances. We were *hauling ass*. About a mile down we were coming up on the Sportsman and I ask him, "What the hell happened back there?"

Out of the blue, he's calm and giving me the Cook's Tour, "Hey. Remember that nurse who did abortions and botched that one in the cabin here?"

"Hey! What happened back at the casino?"

He goes right on, "Remember she cut the woman up and . . .?"

Oh great, I'm thinking, the bastard's gone Section 8. I'm bellowing "What *happened* back there?" and he's going on, blah, blah-blah, blah-blah. ". . . and remember, then she put the head in a bag and . . . ?"

"Hey, Spellbound! What's with the one-track mind? Yes, she stops at the Sportsman for a drink, puts the bag right up on the bar, is getting ready to leave and the bartender reminds her about it. Okay? I remember! " Then I screamed: "*What . . . the . . . fuck . . . happened . . . back there? Remember back there? The Piping Rock?*"

"Sheesh. You don't have to yell. There was a cop car."

I pulled off the road into a driveway and cut the lights. My hands were absolutely shaking. I said in the most sarcastic voice I could muster, "Oh, there was a *cop car* . . ." Then I screamed at him, "That's it? That all? The hell with this. I'm out!" I threw the money in his lap and he threw it back at me, tells me to relax and I told him to go screw himself. I'm out.

"This what you were like under fire?" he asks me. I grabbed his fancy jacket lapel and told him that it helped that what I did in the war was sanctioned by the Navy. I saw a lot of action, served with distinction, and, unlike him, I came out an officer.

He apologized. The only time I really remember him doing that. He said that the cop car wasn't supposed to be there. It was all fixed. "You understand, Mr. Lieutenant?" he asks me. We're back to wiseass. I told him I understand a fix. He tells me to back out and go back down the road toward the Sportsman. He has a cabin near it. Jesus. Then—get this—he turns on the radio. It has a police channel. What next? We pull into the Batcave?

As we swung out, the lights shone on a trailer and he says something like, "Look at that goddamn thing!" And he goes off his rocker about trailers again. He raved about that all the way to the cabin. More trees in New York State than all of Europe and we got our people living in tin cans, busses without wheels. Country's going to hell. Get two generations living in the goddamn things and they'll think it's normal. Back in his day. . .blah, blah, blah.

We pulled in by the cabin. I had a Manhattan in the time it took him . . . him . . . unh, unh. Oh, Jesus. Oh, God, my arm. Oh, Christ, don't me die now. I'm so close. Please God. I'm gonna toss my cookies one of these times and it's gonna be all she wrote.

All right. All right. We're at his cabin. We're in the car waiting. Okay, okay. Unh . . . . Come on, Lord. Stay with me? He throws a carton of Luckies at me and says, "Smoke'em if you got'em."

He tells me everything's set. Patrol car's out there 'cause somebody's grabbing a snooze or a little tail. A little snafu, he calls it. We just wait until they get'im back in action with a fake call. Pheeewwwww. . . . *Damn*, boy. The Spa City police—always there to help.

Well, I'm ashamed to say this. He, uh, he could see . . . see my hands shake as I lit up. Didn't he ever get nervous? Always, he says. *Always* feels like a blivet until he's in there working. "Blivet? I thought you were regular Navy. We zooming back into fairytale time again?"

Wrong thing to say. *Not* for the reason you might think. He takes this *big* breath and I could tell—I-I just *knew* he wanted to give me this long story. Oh, God, and did he. Here's the Readers Digest version. He was on Okinawa with the jarheads. They brought him in from Europe because of his *talents* with jellied gas. He'd have them put delayed charges on canisters of jellied gas, toss'em into the Japs' holes, and ones close to the surface'd run out all on fire and they'd machine gun'em. The rest they found cooked down below. Made him sick to his stomach, he says. Mr. Sensitive. A canister got hit by a stray shell, ignited too close to him and caught his clothes on fire. That was it. The gireens put him out, but they pinned some medals on him and sent him home. He claimed the burn wasn't as extensive as it looked. Yes, doctor. And that thing on Quasimodo's back was only a mole.

Well, he's on'n'on about the jarheads' joys of barbecuing Japs, which I personally think *he* likes, *too*, and all the while I'm just jumping out of my skin. I just couldn't take his crap anymore and just, uh, I just blurted out, "Who're you working for? Why're we doing this? I've been waiting since Willy Lum's!"

"Money, Georgie." Harry the Younger. The Georgie thing again. Then Harry the Elder. Jeckyll and Hyde. "I don't ask questions. I get paid. I do it." Something to that effect. I said, "Cut the shit, mister. I'm thirty-five, not five. It doesn't jibe. They don't hire Harry the Torch to get rid of some sad old casino."

He—now he's Harry the Elder—he gets all huffy. "Don't call me Harry the Torch."

"I'll call you what I want to at this point, Bucky. How about 'imbecile'?" Jesus H. Christ. I'm facing twenty if we get caught and he's worried 'cause I'm not calling him by his Harvard nickname. I pounded on it: "*Why* are we doing this? *Why* are we here? *Who's* hired you?"

"Joe Adonis."

I got really quiet and softly I made a ship to shore sound, "Bee-bee-dee-DEE-dee-dee! Bee-bee-dee-DEE-dee-dee! 'Hello Mr. and Mrs. America. Walter Winchell here. Flash! Joe Adonis hires Harry to torch the Piping Rock.!" I said softly, "God, Harry. Really. I mean, that is so pathetic." *That* pissed him off.

Aungh . . . I ha—have to relax. Easy on me, Lord? Please?

Anyway, he's quiet—thinking I presume—and then he says, "There's evidence there."

"Evidence, schmevidence, Harry." I'm really giving him the full court press. "They pull a Ned and leave the books on the bar," I ask him? Not on the bar, he says. In "special places."

"Books?"

"Jesus Jah-gee. You are *really* dense, dad—like, just not *getting* it? Not books." I made noises that I was still not getting it and he pauses a long pause and says, "A body."

Oh, God. I felt . . . hell, I can't even describe what I felt like. Listen, I've seen bodies. I've done autopsies, hauled the dead and near-dead out of POW camps. But I could've vomited right then and there. My mind's racing. They didn't know this before they sold it?

Quietly he says, "No."

"Who'd be *stupid* enough to hide a body in a casino? I'm screaming again.

He tells me to calm down. "Booze getting to you, Irish? Getting a little nuts?" he wants to know.

"This from a pyro who needs the sports jacket with the wrap around sleeves?" He says in this snotty tone that *he's* an arsonist, *not* a pyromaniac. *I* should know the difference, as a medical man. *He* doesn't *have* to burn things down. *He* does it for a *living*. *He's* not *crazy*! Christ, no. Jonathan

Brewster's not crazy! He's got the Star Suite at Bellevue reserved for him, but *he's* not crazy!

Sorry. I'm rambling. So, Mr. Arsonist asks me if I know Timmy the Tumbler, one of Adonis' boys. Huge lug, I ask? Yup, he says. Has this sad eye on one side? Yup, yup. Has that stupid little broad, the one with the bad dye job—who everybody used to say about, "Dyed blonde hair but a great derriere"? Yup, yup, yup. Then I sure as hell know him. Came in MacFinn's all the time. *Stupid?* He was such a mouth breather he ordered Chapstick by the case. But dangerous? Phewwww . . . . Whelp, seems Timmy screwed up. Didn't dispose of *things* the way they should've been. Once living *things?* Oh, look, look. See bad Timmy. See bad Timmy screw up.

So, I have to ask, if this is Adonis, why not just buy the owner out or muscle in and *take* the building back? Or, if all else fails, then . . . you know? Why? At this point, I swear to God, he goes into the house and brings back a scrapbook—honestly—and says, "I've got books on all of them, Georgie. I document everything and they know it. Now, I don't consider you congenitally stupid, just ignorant." I've used that line a lot since. He says he's going to quote me passages from the 'Book of Kefauver,' as he calls it, and quotes from *New York Times* articles he's got on the Kefauver hearings.

I mean, it was stuff anybody knew, you know? Lansky, Adonis and Costello were the club's co-owners. Ahearn had been on the police force for nineteen years and had never closed up a club. The chief of police knew that cop cars were being used to bring money from the banks to the clubs.

"All right, all right, all right, Harry! Grade schoolers know that! *Big deal!*" I know I'm not getting any further in finding out why we're going to torch this place and all I know for sure is that this son of a bitch will set me up for the fall if I don't. I told him a lot of people knew cop cars took the night money *from* Piping Rock to banks *and* to MacFinn's for the count. None of this makes any difference with him.

"Harry, I smell horseshit piled to the top of your camp. Why are we doing this?" I keep pounding away at him, "*Why?*"

He *explodes* at me and starts yelling, "Why, *why*, **WHY**? Questions, *questions*, **QUESTIONS!**"

"Yes! Yes, you lying bastard! I stand to do *twenty* if we're caught. So, *why?* Why, why, **WHY?**"

"Because *they* want it."

"They? Who 'they?'"

"'They.' The people who can't afford to have *anything* happen that might make them look even remotely involved?" He used schoolteacher tones. I hate when a man does that. "Use your head. Who couldn't afford to do the kind of stuff that Adonis could? It doesn't matter with Adonis. He gets respect if he muscles somebody. Put your thinking cap on, Mr. Chips. Listen, the original name of the place was the Lido Venice, but it was changed to 'Piping Rock.' Where's that name come from? "

His last marble was not just lost—it had *disintegrated*—but I played along. "Like you said, Locust Valley."

Did I actually think, he wanted to know, did I actually, actually think that *mobsters* named a casino "Piping Rock"? That Meyer Lansky or Frank Costello or Joe Adonis named it "Piping Rock"? Did I? "NO," he bellows at me. "The answer's no! It was my people. My people. My people . . . from Locust Valley, the cream of American society." He actually called them that—and was not being sarcastic, mind you. Not at all. They were people his family knew, people his father did business with, sailed with, golfed with. "*My* people. Including Uncle Ned."

Which explained so much, if you think about it. I always thought I was savvy, but, God, I felt stupid right then. *His* people hired Adonis, and the others. Nobody *corrupted* his people. They did it *all* by themselves.

He said I had to understand that he was one of them, but now he was one of them in an even more *special* way, because he was doing the clean-up for them. Honestly, that's what he said. One of *them,* doing the clean up for *all* of them.

I asked him what he'd get. He says, "I get my house back. I get my life back. Or, at least, I get to start over." I looked at my hands and thought to myself, "Dear Jesus, protect me. He's insane." Then he flip-flopped and said none of us can ever start over. I agreed with him on that and pointed out that we were older and it was another time. And he said—and, oh, God, and I will *forever* remember this—he said, no, I didn't understand. It's not another time. It's another country. It's another America, a new America. "This is the third America," he says.

I don't why I didn't just shut him up and drive us away, but like a child I asked, "Third America?"

"It's easy, George. Lincoln had said 'four score and seven years ago' at Gettysburg. The first America began in 1776. Then the second in 1863, eighty-seven years later." And the third America, he says, well, that started in 1945—with a little head start because of the A-bomb.

He didn't say anything for a long minute. I wanted him to stop. I was smoking like a chimney, biting my nails. He was calm. You could tell by the way he smoked. Then he said, get this, he said he and I both grew up in the final days of the second America. Except . . . um . . . except . . . What was it? Uh . . . something like, except that people like him who came of age in the 'twenties knew how good America could be. But children of the 'thirties—like me—we were cheated. Oh yes, I remember that, believe me. "You were all cheated," he said. *Cheated.* We grew up never knowing how good it could be. Now I really wanted him to stop. I didn't want to hear any more of this. He stopped for a couple of seconds, but then he spoke very softly. I couldn't help myself. I was in a trance listening to him. He said, "We don't know what the third America is going to be like, but *I* know how good it *could* be." And then he almost whispered as he said, "And I'm going to have mine."

CHAPTER 15

I slapped it into gear and rolled out, without waiting to know if it was the right time to roll and not caring. I was angry. I was *really* angry. I didn't want to hear *any* of this *any* more. I told him when I went to college I didn't have *time* for philosophy. I didn't have *time* to think about *three* Americas or *Gettysburg* or how *good* it could be.

All he said was, "You know, self pity can kill you."

I said, "Let's get this done."

As we headed back he started taking me through the drill, as much to talk me down as anything. We'd seal off the windows, he says, so there's no li . . . . Unh . . . hang on. Unh . . . I've got to, phew, God, gotta hit the head.

[*Several minutes pass.*] Okay, I'm back. Didn't think I had enough left in me to come up. . . . Hope I have enough tape to finish. Enough tape, enough time. Wish I didn't have to go to work tomorrow. God, it's hard to breathe. Ah, Jennie. Ah, Jennie. Can I stay a little longer? Oh, my God I am heartily sorry for having offended thee . . . .

When we got near enough, I cut the lights and pulled to the side of the road. He went ahead on foot and checked out the situation. He signaled me with a flashlight in semaphore. All clear. I clapped my hands together! Let's get this done! I pulled in with my lights still off through these islands of shrubberies in front of the casino, taking it slow so's not to run over them. I reversed it and backed the Commodore in under the porte cochere at the main door.

He had the key—of course. We brought in these sea bags, filled with cans. I could tell from the sound. I carried more than Harry because of his arm. He shined his flashlight through very quickly and for a minute it was as if we were standing in the old Piping Rock. I was shocked. Everything seemed to be there, but he doused the light so fast I felt I must've been hallucinating. It smelled musty, but it still had that smell bars always do.

He used the light sparingly, just so I could get the seabags over by the front windows. There was some light from the outside, though not much. The aerosol cans were spray paint. Clever bastard. He had me spray the front windows plus any others that could be seen from the road. We did most of them. I thought the fumes would kill us. He had me hold the flash, and he went outside to see where the light leaked. Then we'd spray a bit more.

I could see parts of the club. It was eerie. Harry was all business. Didn't say anything more than he had to. We worked on the windows and he moved fast in spite of his arm. I thought at the time it was getting better. He checked again for light leaks. None. We brought a stand with lights. I did, I mean. It fed off this unbelievable bank of batteries he had in the car. I snuck out to the car and snuck back. It was chilly for mid-August. I was glad to get back in. It was late and all you could hear were the crickets, the occasional car. Standing out there fiddling with the hookup, I'd jump every time I heard one. A car, I mean. Of course, the Meadowbrook was still active at that point, but, Christ, it was a ways across the road. Jesus, what a fool I was.

While we set up the lighting, he went through the drill again, more thoroughly. Felt like I was prepping for a mission. We'd finish wrapping the place. Then, we'd bring in the bottles of vodka and the already-smoked cigarettes. We'd set those up in a couple of areas to make it look like some kids got in and had a joy party, just in case the fire didn't char enough or some junior G-man from the state wasn't aware of certain *arrangements*, shall we say, and went by the book looking for arson. After we were done, we'd take the lights out first, then pack everything, then get ready to pour vodka in one spot, leave piles of empties and the smoked cigarettes in others and ignite everything with his delayed fuses. He'd designed them to look like cigarettes. He was a genius.

Was I ready to roll, he wanted to know? You bet your ass I was. He flipped his lights on and there it was, the Piping Rock, just as I had recalled it. They hadn't done a thing with it. Lord. The tables still even had tablecloths, with set-ups on them. I, I thought it'd be empty. We stood for a brief second staring at it. I was inside a ghost standing next to a ghost. I thought . . . Somebody had tossed some stuff on the floor by one table, otherwise it was as if they'd just walked out and turned the key. We worked our way through it, and it was just same. All the way through. Crap and roulette tables, pictures on the wall, everything, all there. Except booze. The ABC board's strict about that.

I had bent over to pick up a poker chip and he barked at me: "Don't *touch* anything! No souvenirs and no traces of us." I blew him a kiss, gave him a big "sieg heil" and we went to work. I slipped the chip in my pocket. Screw him.

He showed me how to tape what and where. We'd concentrate on the stage where the fire would burn the hottest, although I could see that the whole place'd be a tinder box in no time. We hauled freight, I'll tell you that. I was surprised at how quickly the taping went.

It's hard to describe the stage. There was this sunken area framed by pillars. On the upper landing there were tables and on the lower part was a dance floor, off center and near the orchestra on the east end of the room. The orchestra was on the landing and the stage projected out onto the dance floor by the end of the dance floor. The acts would perform up by the band, sometimes right down on the dance floor. The whole ceiling over it was actually draped cloth or a mesh of some kind that came down tent-like from the center. Gathered, that's what I'm trying to say. Jane said the cloth was that, gathered. Very . . . very elegant.

We were actually standing on the dance floor when I asked where the Tumbler left his, shall we say, *handiwork*. He starts to give me this best-not-to-know crap and I'd had enough of that. "Stow it. I'm here."

He's points down, like this, and says, "*Here*." Suddenly, I didn't really want to know. I mean, Jane and I watched Sophie Tucker sing right there one night, right after the Williams Brothers. We're both standing there and I'm dying for a cigarette and he starts looking around shaking his head up and down, eyes fluttering a little bit. "Yes, indeed, I'm gonna miss this place, George." He saw my look. "Really," he says, "I saw Paul Whiteman walk in one night in 'thirty-seven. Bought him a drink. He actually played my frat dances. Good memories." And he claps his hands together, loud, like this, and says, "Even better memories, I was right at that table when I got the news about Ned." He repeated "Better memories" about a dozen times and I think he actually hummed "Heart of My Heart." You know when somebody still hates somebody who's dead. They have that dry joy in their voice. I've hated some people in my life, but I had to admire the lad. He could have patented the process.

The time on the stage was quiet work—gave me time to think and I didn't want to. I wanted to be done. But, it was like being on the open sea. Your boat's moving across a broad expanse of water. You're always working, but it's rhythmic, almost in time with the waves on the hull, and when you know your job, it leaves you with time to focus on a few different things at once. Now all I was hearing was our footsteps, the crinkle of cellophane and the ripping sound of scotch tape being pulled out in long strips. I started to think about our life in Saratoga. At that point—I'm talking about in 'fifty-four now—I wasn't sorry we left. But after ten years in the Little Loser? Saratoga came to look like heaven. Then I thought about this jackpot, this *onion* of a situation, I was in. Something kept eating at me. But what? Outside of the fact, I mean, that I was taping a building to burn it down? Yes, *thank* you. I was aware of that.

Finally it hit me. Why did *he* stand outside to see if any light was shining through and not *me?* We should have both done it, to be sure. It hit me. "The *dirty* bastard doesn't *trust* me." He was diddling with something'n'his seabag and looked up at me. "Where are you going, George?"

I need more tape, I say. He says he'll get it. "You don't trust me?" I ask him. He hesitates just long enough before saying he does for me to know he doesn't. Which means, from now on, I trust him even less than before. Which was the problem all along. Things didn't jibe—you know? By the time I'm at the car I'm almost talking to myself. T'sall roaring through my head. It's crazy what I'm doing. I'm scared outta my wits and—on *top* of all that—he's got these, these stories.

Where'd I put that beer? "Come to papa, do . . ." Ahhhhhh. . . .

He's got stories inside of stories—the onion. When I see him up in my store, he's supposed to be, what, twenty-eight? And now he's supposed to be *ten* years older than I am? Maybe he's really just a kid who's looney tunes. Maybe his burns are from Korea. Maybe he wasn't in the service *at all.* And then this whole thing with his arm and me coming along and he's *gotta* go to the Brown Log Inn and the second girl *just happens* to be there and I threw his gun in the canal and suddenly he's got a .45 at, at that, at that shitkicker's head? And suddenly, by *accident*—by *accident?*—he's got Tall Dark in on it to blackmail me? And he knows Leary claims I owe him money, but he's claiming he's not here to collect on Leary's debt? But then he's gonna square it with Leary afterwards? And then it's really Adonis and he's torching the Piping Rock for the mob. But then it's *actually* for a group of Long Island snobs he grew up with? Not the mob, just the snobs.

That's all roaring through my head. Sure, I'm up two grand if I *don't* get another penny. But right now, God help me, I would rather be home without the two gees. That's a lot of berries, but not enough for . . . .

So, I'm rummaging in the—he's actually got extra little lights built into the trunk. Just enough light to make me scared shitless that somebody from the Meadowbrook will see something. I mean, I'm not, I'm not thinking rationally. So, I'm searching— I'm searching, all right, I'm searching for a *weapon*. I'm frantic! I can't find the one I stuffed in my pants at the Brown Log Inn. Who the hell knows where that went? I figure he has to have another pistol in this car. I've got a pile of cellophane and scotch tape, just in case hot shot comes out, and I'm pressing on every surface I can find. *Bingo!* A panel pops up. Just fuses. *Damn!* I keep trying. *Bingo* on number two! I could've told without lights on that this is another .45.

I heard his footsteps. I have this hearing you can't believe. He thought he snuck up on me and he hisses, "What the *hell're* you doing out here?"

I pretend I'm startled and hiss back, "Christ! I nearly jumped outta my skin, you stupid fuck!" Something like that, I don't know. I hiss, "Douse the light," while I'm scrambling to hide the .45, put a lot of bravado on, but my heart's in my throat. I knew he had his .45 on'im.

He gets an inch from my face. "What the *hell're* you doing out here, Georgie?"

"What the hell you think I'm doing, Harry? I'm practicing with the band for our final patriotic number of the night, " 'Yank My Doodle, It's a Dandy.' *Get* it?"

"Crack wise and . . ."

"And I'll crack you, if you don't shut up!" I'm trying to stuff the .45 in the back of my pants and I try to distract him by throwing'im a bunch of fuses. Now, he's on my *right*. I throw with my *left* and, son of a bitch, he catches with his right. He grunted, but it was too late—*too late!* His arm's fine. I pretend not to notice, but my mind's racing! "Oh-my-God, oh-my-God! What's *this* all about?" This chill ran down my spine and I tried not to shudder.

Now he tries being the pally-boy again. Uses light talk. "Hey, we're both jumpy. Why don't you grab that last seabag? Hah, hah, hah, hah, hah." That creepy little laugh guys give when they're afraid to fight anymore or they're ready to stick a knife in you. What's in the sea bag? "Cameras," he says. Cameras? Careful, I tell him. Autumn's coming and the squirrels are looking for nuts. He laughs this *ridiculous* laugh. Just, um, pretentious. He sounds like FDR. "Oh, quite hilarious, George."

"'Quite hilarious'?" I thought. God, he must think he's back here in a tux like in the old days—like when Walter Chrysler dropped the four hundred grand in a crap game in 'forty-eight and nonchalantly says," I guess that'll be all for the night, gentleman."

"Come on, George old man," Harry says. "Quite hilarious"? "George old man"? What *is* all this? He's pretending he trusts me so much he turns his back long enough and I get the .45 into my belt. I mean, my pants. You know what I mean.

Back inside everything's ready. The lamp's facing a section of the stage that's very heavily wrapped. He's got 35 mm cameras, and big cameras with huge flashbulbs, like you see crime scene photographers use. He's even got a Polaroid. Just insane.

"What're we doing, Harry?" I ask softly.

"You shoot everything you've done and then you take the last shots with *you* in the picture."

"Oh, that's it. That is *it!* You're gone." I couldn't even hold it in. "You're off your gazipp."

"Georgie, never mind. Let's just take pictures. I've already taken most of the 35 millimeter. Just snap some with me in it."

Georgie again? We're back to Harry Number One? I started praying. God, get me out of this and I'll never screw up again. He sat on the edge of the stage and posed, as if the owner's going to invite him to sing a song. I backed up to a big jardinière that had a dead palm tree in it and dropped the gun in it. I just hoped I could figure how to get back to it. I took the last of the 35 mm film. He looked like he was posing for MGM.

He moved very quickly. I couldn't shut up. Natch. I asked if his arm felt better. He ignored that. He took a bunch of Polaroids and said we'll put the camera by the cigarettes and vodka bottles for an "interesting touch." His words. We took everything else out to the car and stowed it. The big camera he saved for last. He says normally he'd have to set it up on a timer, but he'd have me shoot him. Do you understand what I'm saying? He wanted *me* to shoot his picture. Gave me gloves and a carpenter's pouch, so I could pop the flashbulb out afterward and put it the pouch. Those were huge flashbulbs, not like these little teensy ones like today. Hot, too. Didn't want that to hit the floor and all that cellophane.

First I'm going to shoot one by the bandstand and another by the door. Then, no, it's more fitting for a last shot by the stage. "Fitting." His word. So I snap him by the side door and then we go up by the stage. He's very near a big concentration of cellophane on a chair. I was very near to it and had my leg braced against it, because it was shaking so badly from nerves. I was afraid I'd shake too hard while shooting. I'm watching him through the viewfinder, like a gunnery sight. I felt like one of those photographers who cruise nightclub tables.

He turned around and looks at the place. He was so strange. "I'll miss this place. My favorite carpet joint. Sentimental fool, I guess."

"And, again, I'm taking your picture . . . why?"

He let out this big sigh and gets this professorial voice on him, which makes him sound like FDR giving a lecture. "Why are we taking these shots? Why?" I said that *was* the gist of my question. It's easy, he says. You send them a few positives and let them know that these negatives and *all* the negatives are safe. "They realize photos with *you* in them mean if they screw *you*, you have the means to screw them back. You *always* have to be in the picture. I am *always* in the picture. *Always.*"

He pours out the booze and leaves the bottles by it, some bottles half full. The smell of alcohol is in the air. He puts the fuses and cigarettes by them. "Why're you doing that now?" I ask. So we'll be ready, he says. I put another flashbulb in and I'm aiming when he pulls out his zippo and clicks it open. Before I can say a word, he pulls out his .45.

"Don't even move your hands, George." He steps back. He's got the pistol in his right hand. His injured arm.

Holy Mary Mother of God, he's going to kill me right there. "Oh, Christ, take the goddamn money, if that's it." I start to step forward toward the fuses.

"That's *not* it. Stay there!"

"You're going to kill me."

"I don't *kill* people. I *told* you that. I simply arrange to make situations happen."

He is so strange now. He's ready to touch this thing off and is so excited and here I am, a goddamn distraction. He was young Harry again, probably because he was all antsy like earlier that night. His body was really moving. I was trying to figure out how to get to the pistol. I tried to distract him by getting really mouthy: "Oh, I *love* that. Jesus . . . . 'I simply *arrange* to make situations happen.' I love that."

"I take care of loose ends—loose ends from the old times. Old buildings. Odds'n'ends. Loose ends from the old times. These are new times now and we have to have things tidied up."

"I'm a loose end." Never let it be said Annie's boy was a dullard. "You're going to tidy me up, Harry?" His eyes did that fluttering thing.

"That's *not* my job. Don't move. Just don't move."

"Why?"

"Just don't *move*." He held the .45 straight at me. "And *shut* up!"

I was *laughing*. I had this feeling like I used to when we'd roar in full bore at a Jap destroyer, zigzagging underneath their Eighties until they couldn't aim any lower and we'd be out've range of fire, and drop our torpedoes and zigzag back out and I was so scared and so excited that I'd laugh like a loon and, and sometimes I'd just come in my pants. I looked at him. "Why? Why me? Who am I?"

"Sometimes people just come to know too much . . . ."

"I wouldn't say anything about tonight!"

"Sometimes when people know too much, George, others worry they won't know how to shut up."

"You mean about, about before? I haven't said *anything*. It's over now. Kefauver's three years ago. The state probe's all done a year ago. What others? Those people from Long Island? I don't even know your friends from Long Isl . . . Wait! It's Adonis. It's Adonis! I'm not going to tell anybody we did this. He doesn't ha . . . ."

"*Shut up! Just don't move.*"

He kept the .45 straight at me. I'm a statue on the outside, frantic on the inside. "Why? Why? What do I know that can hurt anybody now?"

"Shhh. You can't talk to me anymore, George."

"It's. No, it's Leary. Is it Uncle Jim? Tell me it's him. Why? Why? He's off the hook! He got acquitted after that witness *mysteriously* disappeared! Is it him? It is, isn't it?" Harry's eyes are narrow, fluttering. "No! It's them. Oh, shit. It is them, right? But, they're not setting this up. They wouldn't do that. They'd have somebody arrange it. Sure. Sure. But who? Who is it? *Who's setting this up for them?* **Who?** I mean, Jesus, Harry. You can at least tell me who's setting this up. At least give me that."

Quietly he said, "Meyer Lansky."

"Oh, Harry! Harry, are, are you absolutely nuts? I don't know him! I don't know Meyer Lansky!" Harry shrugs and does that thing with his mouth that says he's not buying it. My mind is racing. Why would Harry think I—oh shit! You mean . . . what I'd said about Proser? Harry, you don't think I know Lansky just because I knew Proser, do you?"

"Knowing Proser. And staying at the Warwick, George? Meyer's favorite hotel? A pharmacist? A pharmacist knows the manager? A pharmacist knows Proser? Come on . . . ."

"Harry! For Christ's sake! It's me. Look at me! Look. You're right. I *am* just a pharmacist, but I . . . ."

He lifts the .45 and aims at me. "They just can't have little pharmacists, knowing what they know, knowing what they know . . . ."

"Jesus, Harry! I'm George . . . ."

He's plowing right on, "*Knowing* who they know, knowing *what* they know, in such deep trouble. So deeply troubled."

"Harry . . ."

He cocks the .45 and aims it right it at my head. His voice is flat. His eyes are dead. "I said 'Shhh.' Damn, Georgie. I like you too much."

It must have been my nerves. The camera suddenly flashes, but I know definitely what I'm doing next, because I pop that big hot bulb right out onto that pile of cellophane and vodka and **BOOM!** It's a ball of flames and a shot's ringing by me and Harry screaming, "No. It's not time yet!" and there's the noise of burning and I scream back "For you to kill me?" And suddenly I'm running and the place is suddenly just *blazing* and *roaring* and he's screaming, screaming, "You . . . can't . . . run . . . George!" But I *am* running and I run backwards and fall and get up and scramble up steps to the landing. Now that canopy is ablaze like incendiary flares in the war and I don't know where the hell to go and I'm banging into tables and groping the wall off the side of the stage trying to find a door and **WHOOM** there's another roar and it's like hideous screaming and I am praying "Please, God, please get me out of here, please. Please, please, God, please get me out of here, please. Holy Mary Mother of God pray for us sinners!" **BANG!** A **HUGE** explosion—**whoom!**—and I am on my knees and I have cuts all over my hands and I'm screaming and crying "I am in hell I am in hell I am in hell!"

I have my necktie stuffed in my mouth. Everything is sunlight bright, searingly hot from the flames and the smoke. I know my eyes will be scorched. I'm really low on the floor, hell, I'm crawling and I get to the wall where there's this door and I lunge at it and it bursts open! Air rushing in causes another explosion. I go down—it blows me out the door—but I get right up. I can see now that I'm out back and I head around to the front for the car. And you know what? I still have that *goddamn camera* in my hand!

I didn't even have the car door closed and I was on my way out. I was *moving*. Then, all of a sudden, out of *nowhere*, a huge Caddie rounds the corner! God, what the hell's *that doing* there! I screamed something at it—I, I, I can't remember—and I floored it. My Studebaker all but stood up. I hit that Caddie at *Christ* knows what speed! All that weight beneath me just shot it aside like it was a toy. It went up on two wheels and I think it tipped over. I was on Gilbert then out on Union in seconds and hit that gas, cranked that wheel and took *off!* And I did not look back.

CHAPTER 16

I drove like a bat out of hell and took every little side road I knew. My heart was pounding in my ears. Nobody was going to find *me*. Nobody knows back roads the way I do. I found a spot on the other side of Saratoga Lake and parked. I just sat there. It took me—what?—five, maybe ten minutes to stop shaking. I was . . . so . . . angry. I was . . . so . . . so goddamn . . . angry. I got the thermos out. I sipped it. I didn't want to go into shock. I needed to gather my thoughts. Oh, my God, my mind was racing. The fire. Meyer Lansky. They tell Lansky? They? They who? I was so scared. What was I going to do? You lying bastard, Harry. You said you weren't going to kill me and then you're shooting at me? You insane lying bastard. And questions, puzzles, are firing like flares in my mind. How'd that fire start so fast? It tore through that canopy! Just, just ripped through it! We didn't tape that! Who was in the Caddie? Did Harry have somebody in another car and they tried to head me off? The lying bastard. The dirty, lying bastard.

Well, I wasn't there twenty minutes and I knew one thing, I needed protection. And I figured I had it. *Right* in those cameras. I had to get that film developed. I knew someone who could do it. I drove somewhere, I won't say where, and I went to someone's house. I won't say who. I woke him up and stuffed a thousand dollars in his hands and said he had to do this and never tell anybody. I wanted everything developed and prints made from the big camera. I would get everything, positives and negatives, and he would never say anything. Could he do that for a grand? He said he could.

I ransacked the Studebaker while he was working. I found more money, plus pistols, pump shotguns, machine guns, hand grenades. Jesus. Patton's Third in one car.

It was a long time before my friend came out to me. He was shaking. He gave me an envelope and said it had the negatives and duplicate prints from the big camera and told me he hadn't developed the rest of it. Hadn't even taken the film out of the cameras. He told me to take the stuff and the money and get out and never talk to him again about it. He was shaking badly. He tried to give me the money back, but I wouldn't take it. Instead I gave him *another* thousand. Hell, there was enough in that car. I looked at him and said, "You never saw me. I never saw you." I always liked him.

I put the smaller cameras back where Harry'n'I had packed them, but I kept the big one and the envelope next to me. I didn't know where else to go so I drove home. Better for me to be there, I thought. I parked the car down to the rear of the store where I could see it. I left the keys in it. I took the pistols inside and left the drawers open so Harry'd know I had'em. I sat in the prescription room and waited. I kept an eye on the car down in the lot.

It took me awhile—I don't why, but it did—but I finally got the courage to open the envelope and look at the prints. Right there in the top one was Harry, holding the gun on me. In back of Harry was a man pointing a gun at me. Son of a bitch. Harry wasn't lying. He didn't kill people. He was just holding on to me until somebody else came to punch my dance card.

I figured I'd better let Harry know I knew, so he could tell Lansky and "the others"—his society buddies—who didn't want me around anymore. I got a big envelope and slipped a photo inside, this one showing just Harry. Harry all alone, just smiling, all alone in the shot with the cellophane glistening in the background. I put the envelope on the seat of the car with a typed note tucked inside that said, "The negative is safe. It isn't here, but it will show up if I don't show up." Actually, that was crap. But how would he know—they know?

It was almost dawn. I was standing by the large door that looked down on the car. One person came up to it, looked around for a minute or so and drove away. "Yeah. Run away, Harry, you coward." Honestly? I was glad he did.

I had a lot of explaining to do with Jennie and finally lied and said I'd come back from the Manhattan and fell asleep in the prescription room. That seemed to do the trick. She called me a stupid Irish bastard and I knew I was okay.

I got a call later that day. The voice was muffled, but I understood, "Hey, Dad. You really banged up my car. Thanks for the photos. Be seeing you." I started to say something but the line went dead. God, I was never so scared, not even at the Piping Rock the night before.

I waited for something, somebody. I waited for him.

I sat and thought about it. Thought hard. I ran what he said over and over in my mind. He never asked about the guns or the big camera. Why? It didn't make sense. He knew I had the big camera.

I waited. Time went by. Just so you know, I never got another call. Never. The *Saratogian* had a huge story about the fire—you know, the public story? Big weenie roast, causes unknown, and all that sort of razzmatazz. The *Saratogian* had a front page shot of it fully involved. Amazing how they got there so soon. Yeah, the whole thing was typically Saratoga—a successful fire with everybody winking at each other saying, "Oh, my goodness, what a surprise!" It certainly was for the poor bastard who'd bought the place. But, *caveat emptor*, right Harry?

But, no, I never heard a word. It was over. Anyway, that's what I let myself think. Although it took about a year to climb down from all that. I never heard a noise that I didn't . . . didn't . . . just give me a minute to pull myself together. Phew . . . .

Okay. Let's end this. Let's wrap it up. Three years later—no, not even three, because it was January of 'fifty-seven—anyways, in January of 'fifty-seven the citizens of the fair City of Saratoga Springs were treated to a spectacular blaze, courtesy of "an arsonist unknown." A good chunk of Broadway was lost in that bonfire. My old store . . . Jesus . . . my old store, MacFinn's, went up. A few days after it, I got an envelope. It was hand delivered one night to the Little Loser. I never heard or saw a soul. I came out to close up and there it was—just propped up on the cash register, no postmarks, nothing except my name on the outside and the word "Confidential" typed on it. Inside there were several black and white photos of the interior of MacFinn's. I looked around for a minute at my little store, then back at those. They were, um, excellent . . . excellent shots of most of the interior, sections all wrapped in what I knew was cellophane. It was, well, very obvious. I had seen that wrapping firsthand and, boys'n'girls, MacFinn's wasn't being wrapped as a present. God.

I felt a cold, sick feeling in my stomach. I stuffed the photos back in the envelope, ran around and shut off all the lights, and locked the door. I searched the store to see if anyone else was there. There wasn't. I had some coffee left and I sat in the dark at the counter and smoked for a minute. My breathing was so shallow, I can feel it now. I had to pull myself together.

I took everything and went out back to the prescription room and stood by the desk by the old safe. There was a typed note attached to the photos. All it said was, "Thought you'd like a souvenir of my handiwork—a keepsake for old times." I stared at them long and hard. Then I sat down. I was shaking. Was it starting all over? Was *he* starting all over? Was he coming back? Or was *someone* coming back? Coming back to finish unfinished business? Or maybe, at least, maybe to blame all this new fire on me somehow?

I'd pick up the photos, look at them and then put them back down. I looked at them over and over and *over*. I'd only run MacFinn's about five years, but so much of my life was in that photo. I looked at the soda fountain, the balcony, and in my mind's eye I saw them all—all the people I worked with—like they were in the photo. God, I remember saying to myself, "I was such a kid when I came here." Twenty-eight. And now, here I was, thirty-eight and looking at that empty store like it was a hundred years ago in my life.

And that's when it hit me. That empty store. I knew that store. And I knew Harry. I went and I got a magnifying glass and I looked at the photos under the light. I must've gone over those shots a hundred times already, but this time I really looked. And I saw it. Actually, it was what I *didn't* see. There was nobody in any of those photos. *Nobody.* Just the store, all wrapped up in cellophane like a Whitman's twenty pound sampler. It was empty. No people. *No* one. Get it? *No person was in the photo.* Right then and there I *knew*—Harry hadn't set that fire. Whoever took those photos had broken Harry's cardinal rule. "I am *always* in the picture." That's what he said. "I am *always* in the picture. *Always.*"

And in a heartbeat I knew . . . I *knew*, I *knew* right then and there that he had never left Piping Rock alive that night. I played that night back in my head. I understood now. I understood it all now. They never meant to kill *me* . . . never meant to kill *me*. He thought they did. When he screamed, "No. It's not time yet!" he was screaming at them that, somehow, the timing was off. And then when he said, "You can't run, George!" he didn't say that. He, he didn't sa . . . . Help me, Lord God, it's hurting so *much*! [*Deep gasping breaths.*]

It's not what he said. I heard it again now in my mind. It was *different*. I heard his words again. Do you understand me? *Do you understand me?* He was saying, "You can't! Run, George!" He was telling me to *run*! Do you understand me? He was telling *me— me! He was telling me to run! To run!*

They didn't even care about *me*. I went and got the other photo—the last photo—I'd taken at Piping Rock in 'fifty-four, just before the fire started. I looked at it again. That guy with the gun wasn't pointing at *me* . . . now that I really, really looked at it. He wasn't pointing at me. Wasn't even pointing at *me*! He was pointing the goddamn gun at Harry. He was there to kill Harry. Harry knew it when he screamed "You can't!" He was screaming at *them*! And he was realizing it was all a set up and telling me to run! Jesus, Jesus, Jesus, Jesus, Jesus . . . .

I don't know. Maybe he wasn't. I don't know . . . I, I think maybe if it'd gone all right they might've killed me. Maybe. No, probably would've had to—to clean things up. But, it didn't . . . didn't go all right and I escaped. I was lucky. They didn't come for me. I was lucky . . . .

Lucky? Aw, Jesus, who am I kidding? *Come on, George! Lucky?* They weren't going to come after me and kill me. I was such small potatoes. I knew it—I knew they figured—unh, oh, my chest, God—I knew they figured I'd be too fucking scared to say anything. And . . . goddamn'em, they were right. They were right. Goddamn them, they were right. [*He is crying here.*]

And three years had gone by and I thought I'd escaped. And MacFinn's and Broadway burns down and they send me some photos. For what reason? Just to keep scaring me? Maybe even have me thinking they can tie me in with this one? Because they knew me. They knew I wouldn't call the cops'n'tell'em that I'd been drawn in like some *sucker?* That I'd gone to Piping Rock just as a stupid shill, just so, so they could kill him? Tell the cops I was just *bait* to distract Harry so they could just, just . . . kill him? Because *he* was the loose end. *You* were the loose end, Harry. *You* were. They couldn't trust *you* to keep quiet, couldn't trust you wouldn't want more. *You* were the loose end. You just kept wanting to have things back the way they were and that just wasn't going to happen. We all want that and it won't happen. It wasn't going to happen and you couldn't get it through your head that they used me to stop you until it was too late. Lord have mercy on my soul. Lord have . . . mercy . . Christ have mercy . . . . I never meant to be . . . I never meant . . . . I never wanted that . . . I . . . .

So, you finally got it, Harry? *Damn it! Didn't you?* You got it was all just a play, just a play, you poor dumb bastard, Harry. They got you to rope me into helping you and, poor Harry, you were thinking *you* were pulling *me* in, for *them* to kill *me*. And even after I screwed up their little summer stock production by popping the flashbulb out and starting everything too soon and then getting away, they figured I'd be too scared ever to say anything. Like the scared little rabbit. Figured *I* wouldn't say anything. No need to kill Georgie, huh? Be too messy. Oh, Georgie'll keep quiet about it all. The scared little rabbit will keep quiet about it all. And they were right. They were right.

[*There is a long period where he just sobs uncontrollably.*]

Oh, oh, oh, oh . . . I want to cry forever. Jennie, I am so scared. I don't want to die.

Shit. Listen to me! Like some old man!

I sat for a long time looking at that photo I'd taken in 'fifty-four, then the newer one I had just gotten. The scared little rabbit looked back'n'forth'n'back'n'forth'n'back'n'forth. I must have chain-smoked a pack of cigarettes. I looked at Harry. He was, he was . . . what? Defiant? Yes. Defiant. He was defiant in those shots. Funny, I . . . didn't hate him anymore. He'd tried to save me. He had, really. Poor bastard. "Thanks, Harry," I said to the photo. For giving me a second . . . . [*A long period of uncontrolled crying.*]

Okay. Okay. So, I said out loud to myself, "What'd they do with him?" Did they just bulldoze what was left of him into the cellar of the Piping Rock? Or maybe they didn't want to take a chance and took his charred bits over to the Hudson and dumped him in. It wasn't rational, but it seemed that was probably the more likely of the two. No chances. I thought about Harry, floating down the Hudson, coming so near to Oyster Bay, but never getting there . . . just floating on past and out to sea.

Give me a second . . . . Give me a second. Oh, Lord . . . . Oh, Lord . . . . [*There is a long period of intermittent crying and silences.*]

So, so . . . God . . . . So, I sat there and, well, I began to fume—first at myself, then at them. And then I thought, *screw* them, screw *all* of them— but, especially, screw him. There may have been a group, that group of *them*, his society pals—and Adonis and Costello and Lansky—but I knew who was at the heart of all this. Goddamn right I did. I knew who pulled the strings. I sat there looking at that photo. I asked it—I asked Harry—who ran the machine in Saratoga? Who ran the Republican machine in the county? Huh? *Huh, Harry?* Who was both a respectable lawyer and a mob lawyer? Who knew Adonis and Costello and Lansky? *Knew them?!* Shit! Did business with them! Raked in Piping Rock take with them and with your Locust Valley crowd every season, Harry? Your *cream* of American society, Harry? *Cream* of American society. Don't make me puke. Who sold your *cream* their bennies and blue heavens, and got them their abortions and kept them all at arm's length from the mob, so they could be bad and be safe at the same time? Who, *Harry? Who?*

Well, I knew who. Mm-hm. Oh, I knew who very well, I did. I should have. I worked for that old boy. I did all of his shit work. They always said he was a spider. He could pull all the strings and make everything burn, and never get caught in the flames. He'd arrange for everything *they* wanted and everybody would owe him. And nobody could ever touch him.

Well, I'd touch him. I'd let *him* know *I* knew. I'd let *him* know I knew that Harry never sent that note—*could never even* have sent that note, because he wasn't even alive in nineteen fifty-seven! I decided I'd write another note, just like I did in 'fifty-four, but this time—*this* time—I'd send it direct and—this time?—this time I'd send it with the other shot from the Piping Rock that night, that one I took with Harry **and** the guy holding the gun on Harry. Uh-huh. I'd let him see now that we *all* knew—*all* of us. Him, them, me, *all* of us. Let him see that we were all in the picture . . . hah, hah, hah. Let him see that *I* had *him* just like he thought *he* had *me*.

I went over to the counter and stuck a sheet of the pharmacy's letterhead in it, and I typed a little note, just like Harry would've done. And very carefully I said—and oh, I remember these words—very carefully I said to him:

> "Dear Uncle Jim,
>
> Just a note to say that the negative <u>for this 'group shot' and all the rest of the negatives</u> are safely tucked away. Just as Harry would have done, if he could have. Which he couldn't. And we both know why. You slipped the key to some other Harry and had him sneak into the store in the wee hours, long after the staff was gone. You had him gift wrap the store, just as Harry would have, and then take pretty photos, just like Harry. But you really should have taken your time and looked at all the other photos from those other jobs you had Harry do. Or, maybe you did and thought I wouldn't notice. I noticed.
>
> I knew you'd want to know. I'm here if you want to have a chat.

And I underlined "for this 'group shot' and all the rest of the negatives." And I took a pen and signed it, "Love, George." The next day I sent it out Special D. And I waited.

And I never heard another word.

Never another word.

Never.

[Here there is a long period of silence, broken by steady breathing, and what sounds like a person smoking. Finally, the silence is broken:]

I think I'll go to the Queensbury next weekend.

Afterward

The tape was shut off immediately after that. Nothing more was recorded about the Piping Rock or about anything else. On that following weekend George A. King went to the Queensbury Hotel in Glens Falls, New York. It would be his last visit to a place he loved. He died not quite a week after that visit, on the night of Thursday, July 30 or early morning Friday of July 31, 1987, in his apartment. He had suffered a massive heart attack on the stairs leading up to his apartment, but had managed to reach his bedroom, where he died. The next morning he failed to show up at work. He was found dead at the side of his bed, kneeling, with his hands clasped tightly, as if in prayer. On the stand next to the bed was *The Merck Manual of Diagnosis and Therapy*, which he had bookmarked.

jack

Don't worry, don't worry. Look at the Astors and the Vanderbilts, all those big society people. They were the worst thieves - and now look at them. It's just a matter of time.

Meyer Lansky